FIGHTING WORDS

Y OU AIN'T SO tough." The long-haired one
wanted to swagger a little. "We're going to kill
both you and him."

They were talking up a killing and Flint did not
wait for them to get ready. He shot the long-haired
one through the stomach.

His draw was unexpected. They had expected him
to talk, perhaps to try to talk them out of it. They
were expecting words and he gave them lead. He
drew and fired so swiftly it caught them flat-footed.

The man he had shot sat very still, then slid from
the saddle and hit the ground with a small thud.

Flint looked through the curl of smoke from his
gun. "All right. Who's next?"

Bantam Books by Louis L'Amour

NOVELS

Bendigo Shafter
Borden Chantry
Brionne
The Broken Gun
The Burning Hills
The Californios
Callaghen
Catlow
Chancy
The Cherokee Trail
Comstock Lode
Conagher
Crossfire Trail
Dark Canyon
Down the Long Hills
The Empty Land
Fair Blows the Wind
Fallon
The Ferguson Rifle
The First Fast Draw
Flint
Guns of the Timberlands
Hanging Woman Creek
The Haunted Mesa
Heller with a Gun
The High Graders
High Lonesome
Hondo
How the West Was Won
The Iron Marshal
The Key-Lock Man
Kid Rodelo
Kilkenny
Killoe
Kilrone
Kiowa Trail
Last of the Breed
Last Stand at Papago Wells
The Lonesome Gods
The Man Called Noon
The Man from Skibbereen
The Man from
  the Broken Hills
Matagorda
Milo Talon
The Mountain Valley War
North to the Rails
Over on the Dry Side
Passin' Through
The Proving Trail

The Quick and the Dead
Radigan
Reilly's Luck
The Rider of Lost Creek
Rivers West
The Shadow Riders
Shalako
Showdown at Yellow Butte
Silver Canyon
Sitka
Son of a Wanted Man
Taggart
The Tall Stranger
To Tame a Land
Tucker
Under the
  Sweetwater Rim
Utah Blaine
The Walking Drum
Westward the Tide
Where the Long Grass
  Blows

SHORT STORY COLLECTIONS

Beyond the Great
  Snow Mountains
Bowdrie
Bowdrie's Law
Buckskin Run
The Collected Short
  Stories of Louis
  L'Amour (vols. 1–7)
Dutchman's Flat
End of the Drive
From the Listening Hills
The Hills of Homicide
Law of the Desert Born
Long Ride Home
Lonigan
May There Be a Road
Monument Rock
Night over the Solomons
Off the Mangrove Coast
The Outlaws of Mesquite
The Rider of
  the Ruby Hills
Riding for the Brand
The Strong Shall Live
The Trail to Crazy Man
Valley of the Sun
War Party

West from Singapore
West of Dodge
With These Hands
Yondering

SACKETT TITLES

Sackett's Land
To the Far Blue Mountains
The Warrior's Path
Jubal Sackett
Ride the River
The Daybreakers
Sackett
Lando
Mojave Crossing
Mustang Man
The Lonely Men
Galloway
Treasure Mountain
Lonely on the Mountain
Ride the Dark Trail
The Sackett Brand
The Sky-Liners

**THE HOPALONG CASSIDY
  NOVELS**

The Riders of High Rock
The Rustlers of West Fork
The Trail to Seven Pines
Trouble Shooter

NONFICTION

Education of a
  Wandering Man
Frontier
The Sackett Companion:
  A Personal Guide to
  the Sackett Novels
A Trail of Memories:
  The Quotations of
  Louis L'Amour,
  compiled by
  Angelique L'Amour

POETRY

Smoke from This Altar

LOST TREASURES

Louis L'Amour's Lost
  Treasures: Volume 1
No Traveller Returns

FLINT

A NOVEL

Louis L'Amour

BANTAM BOOKS
NEW YORK

2019 Bantam Books Mass Market Edition

Published in the United States by Bantam Books,
an imprint of Random House, a division of
Penguin Random House LLC, New York.

BANTAM BOOKS and the HOUSE colophon are
registered trademarks of Penguin Random House LLC.

Originally published in paperback in the United States by
Bantam Books, an imprint of Random House, a division of
Penguin Random House LLC, in 1960.

ISBN 978-0-553-25231-6
Ebook ISBN 978-0-553-89915-3

Map: Alan McKnight
Cover art: Gregory Manchess
Photograph of Louis L'Amour: John Hamilton—Globe Photos, Inc.

Printed in the United States of America

randomhousebooks.com

80

Bantam Books mass market edition: March 2019

FLINT

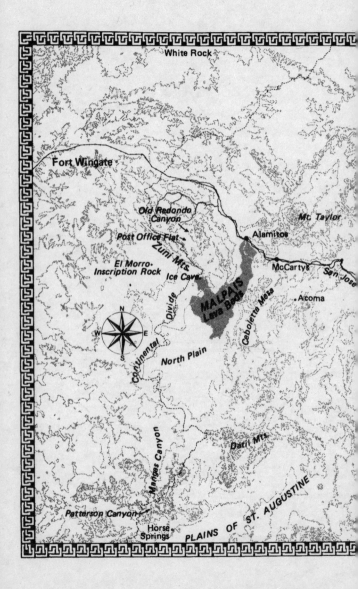

Santa Fe ●

Railroad

Rio Grande

**WEST CENTRAL
NEW MEXICO**
Contour Intervals 500 feet
MILES
0   10   20   30

Socorro ●

UTAH   ● Leadville   Missouri R.
                                  Abilene ● Kansas City
Colorado R. COLORADO Arkansas R. KANSAS

ARIZONA   Dodge

              Santa Fe ● PUBLIC LAND
              AREA OF   Tascosa ● Canadian R. INDIAN
Tonto   DETAIL
Basin   MAP   TERRITORY
              NEW MEXICO
Silver City ● ● Lake Valley   Sulphur R. TEXAS

              ● El Paso ● Cheyenne

                    MEXICO

CHAPTER 1

IT IS GIVEN to few people in this world to disappear twice but, as he had succeeded once, the man known as James T. Kettleman was about to make his second attempt.

If he did not succeed this time he would never know it, for he would be dead.

When a man has but a few months to live, he can, if he so wills, choose the manner of his going, and Kettleman had made such a choice. He was now on his way to a place of which he alone knew, and there he would die. He would die as he had lived—alone.

It was ironic that he who hated the West should return there to die, but like a wild animal which knows when death is upon it, he was seeking a dark and lonely place where he could die in peace, and in his own way.

At this moment no man in the railroad car looked stronger, more alive, more resolute, yet the seed of death was in him and the plant had but a little while to grow.

There were five people in the car. The lights were dim, the passengers lay sprawled in uncomfortable sleep. The train rushed westward through the cold, clear night, carrying the man steadily toward his final destination.

A very pretty young woman, who had got on at

Santa Fe, sat a few seats ahead of him and across the aisle. Farther front, three men were seated, each traveling alone. Occasionally the conductor entered, accompanied by a blast of cold air. Several times he added fuel to the cast-iron stove.

People interested Kettleman only as prospective antagonists, and of the men in the car only one seemed likely to fit that category. He was a strawhaired man with a lean and dangerous look, like a wolf among sheep.

The girl was tall, gracefully slender, and her brown eyes had a way of looking directly at a man that was frank without boldness. Kettleman decided she was a girl who had been much around men, that she was used to them and liked them. Her name was Nancy Kerrigan. He overheard it when she was giving directions for packages to be placed in the baggage car.

The country outside was invisible. The windows had steamed over, and the train moved as if through an endless tunnel. To Kettleman it did not matter, for he knew every foot of this roadbed and the surrounding country from descriptions which had come to his desk in New York.

The high plain was broken at intervals with long ridges and outcroppings of lava, and in the mountains there was marketable timber. When he began planning his second disappearance, Kettleman had gone over all available reports and maps.

They were climbing steadily. Ahead were high mesas, more lava, and occasional ruins. Soon the train would slow for a long, steep grade. When that time came he would step off the train into the darkness.

His destination was familiar only from a description given him fifteen years ago, over a campfire, by a man who had often used the place for a hideout. When he left the train he would return to the oblivion from which he had emerged fifteen years earlier.

Then James T. Kettleman would cease to exist—although actually he had ceased to exist a few days ago, in Virginia. For the few weeks that remained to him he would be nameless once more.

To disappear the first time had been relatively easy for the lanky, seventeen-year-old youngster he was then.

No one noticed him when he came into the saloon at The Crossing that night with Flint. It was not until the brief silence that followed the blasting of guns that their attention was drawn to him by the cocking of his gun.

The men who killed Flint had scarcely seen the boy until that moment, but, within the space of five seconds, five of them were shot dead and two were dying. Two more were wounded, but would live to carry the memory of that shocking five seconds to their graves.

And in the darkness after the lights had been shot out, the boy had carried Flint from the room.

There was a doctor at an Army post twenty miles away, but they were never to make it.

Legend was born that night in Kansas, and the story of the massacre at The Crossing was told and retold over many a campfire. Neither the man at the card table nor the youngster who carried him away was known, and both vanished as if the earth had opened to receive them.

The events preceding the shooting provided only

the information that two roughly dressed men had come in out of the night, and one bought chips in a poker game while the other dozed near the door. This was the youngster who, upon that night, was to shoot himself into western history.

The man at the table played a shrewd, intelligent game, and at the end of two hours he was winner by a small amount. The first indications of trouble came from the bar where a group of Texas trail drivers were drinking.

The trail drivers had noticed the stranger playing cards and, after some whispering among them, they had drifted over to gather around the table. Suddenly two of the trail hands grabbed the stranger's arms, and one of the others said, "This man is a hired killer." Then four of the trail drivers fired into his body.

In the instant of silence that followed the shooting they heard the click of a drawn-back gun hammer, and every head turned. "He was my friend," the youngster said, and he started shooting.

Of the five killed in the first blast, four died from head shots, all fired in the split seconds before somebody shot out the lights.

Of the two survivors, neither would talk, but one of the dying men had whispered, "Flint!" It was rumored that Flint was the name of an almost legendary killer who was occasionally hired by big cattle outfits or railroad companies.

The train whistled, the lonely sound trailing off across the windswept plains. Kettleman got out his pipe and lighted it. His two bags and haversack were at the back of the car. When he opened that door there would be a moment when the cold air might awaken the others, but he would be gone.

Up to a point he had planned every move, but once arrived at Flint's old hideout there would be nothing to do but wait. Some time ago his doctor told him he would not live a year, and most of that year had passed.

He sat in what was called a parlor car, because of its elaborate lamp fixtures and narrow strips of mirror between the windows. In one of these he glimpsed himself.

His face was lean and hard, triangular, with high cheekbones, green eyes, and a strong jaw. His sideburns were long in the fashion of the time, his hair dark brown and curly. In the light it showed a tinge of red. His skin was dark, his features, except for his eyes, normally without expression.

James T. Kettleman, financier and speculator, had often been called a handsome man. He had never been called a friendly one.

In the fifteen years since leaving Kansas he had not been west of the Appalachians until now.

There had been more than fifteen hundred dollars in Flint's pockets when he died on that rain-soaked Kansas hillside, following the shooting at The Crossing. The boy who was to become James T. Kettleman had sixty dollars of his own, which he used to buy an outfit of store clothes in Kansas City.

He traveled to New York and sold his four horses for an additional four hundred dollars. With this stake he started in business. It was more money than either Jay Gould or Russell Sage had started with.

The name Kettleman was a switch on "cattleman,"

a name invented for him by Flint when the boy entered school. He had never had a name of his own.

The train whistled and he got to his feet and stretched, the movement drawing the attention of the young woman. "It is some distance to Alamitos," she told him.

When he smiled his face lighted up. "It isn't the stations one has to worry about," he said, "it's the side tracks."

He caught her puzzled glance, and smiled again, strolling to the back of the car where he rubbed the steam from the window and looked out, seeing the scattered stars, and grass bending before the wind. On the edge of the embankment there was snow.

Nancy Kerrigan was disturbed by the comment, yet she thought of its truth. So many people became sidetracked and missed the things that were worthwhile. Maybe she herself was one of them. She glanced at the man again. He did not look like a western man, yet he did. He was a striking man, but he looked lean and savage.

James T. Kettleman returned to his seat and sat down. Another ten minutes...

In the fifteen years following that night at The Crossing he had built his small stake to many millions, making many enemies and no friends in the process. He married a wife who tried to have him killed, and had no children.

Now he was stepping out of that life as he had stepped into it, leaving nothing behind that mattered. Nor would he take anything with him, not even a memory that he cared to keep.

Thirty years earlier, when he was two years old, he

had been picked from the brush near a burned wagon train, where he had been overlooked by raiding Comanches. There were no other survivors. Nothing remained to tell who he was, and those who found him had no interest in learning. During the next four years he was handed around from family to family and finally abandoned on a cold night in a one-street western town.

Kettleman walked to the rear of the car again, glancing back at the occupants. All were asleep, or apparently asleep. The train was slowing for the long climb. Lifting his bags through the rear door he closed it carefully behind him. The stars blinked coldly from an almost clear sky, the train whistled, the wind blew long across the high grass plains.

He threw his bags to the roadbed and put a leg over the rail, hesitating one brief instant to look back into the dimly lighted car. This was the end of everything and the beginning of nothing. He put the other leg over the rail and dropped to the roadbed.

He stood watching the red lights on the back of the train, which moved away, scarcely faster than a man could walk, until it rounded a curve and left no more than a humming of the rails to tell of its passing, and the long whistle of the locomotive echoing down the night sky.

The dry grass bent before the wind, and seed pods rattled in the brush along the right of way.

James T. Kettleman was ended, and the man who had borne that name, making it feared and respected, stood now where he had stood so many years before, without a name. He was now a man without a past as he had been a boy without one.

"Good-bye," he said, but there was nobody to say the word to, and nothing to remember.

Slinging the haversack over his shoulders, he retrieved the two bags and, climbing from the shallow cut where the track ran, he started off across the plain toward a high, comblike ridge, crested with trees.

A sharp pain struck him suddenly and he stopped abruptly, bending far over and retching violently. He dropped to his knees, caught by a sudden weakness, and remained there, frightened at the agony. He had never known physical pain—although often hunger—and anything that robbed him of strength left him shaken, for his strength was all he had. Now, here at the end, he needed it desperately.

Later there would be more pain, but in the last days, his doctor had said, there would be less of it.

Among the pines he searched for and found a hollow protected from the wind. He broke twigs from the lower trunks of the trees and built a small fire. He found a deadfall which he dragged nearer to use for a windbreak. With a razor-sharp bowie knife, he cut limbs to hold the fire. He took a kettle from his gear and put on water for coffee. He changed into jeans, a wool shirt, and a sheepskin coat. He put on flat-heeled hiking boots and got out his two pistols, one of which he belted on.

The pistols were Smith & Wesson .44 Russians, and the best gun built. He thrust the second gun into his waistband. Out of the longer case he took a high-powered custom-made rifle and assembled it, then a shotgun.

He made a bed on pine boughs, spreading a thin ground sheet and blankets atop the boughs. He loaded the remaining clothing, food, and ammunition into the big haversack. With his gear packed, the load weighed over eighty pounds.

Then he warmed some soup and drank it, and the gnawing pain in his stomach subsided a little. He carried the two bags into the woods and buried them under some thick brush.

A searching wind prowled the forest, far-off a faint call sounded, and a shot. He listened, but the sound faded.

From a few yards off in the brush his fire was not visible, and he was pleased. He gathered more fuel, removed his boots, and crawled into his bed.

Every move of his disappearance had been carefully prepared. Fortunately he had dealt largely in cash and always kept large quantities of it available. Quietly he had transferred some funds, shifted stock from one company to another, and made arrangements to cover every need in case he should live longer than expected.

On a trip to his Virginia farm he had consulted an attorney in Baltimore, a former Supreme Court judge. Drawing up a will, he followed it with a carefully prepared document for the management of his affairs.

"I shall go away," he explained, "as I have learned I have but a short time to live. If, after seven years, I have not returned I will naturally be declared legally dead and my affairs can be settled."

"And if you die before that length of time?"

"I want nothing done until after seven years. As you will see, I have provided for my wife."

"For a man of your means," the judge suggested, "it is very little."

"This I have not mentioned to anyone, nor do I want it mentioned, but last week in Saratoga my wife tried to have me killed—my wife and her father. You will find the reports from the Pinkerton Agency and my own statement among the papers in my safe-deposit box."

"There is divorce."

"They would fight it, and I might not live long enough. Also, I believe they will try again to have me killed, for I have not told them how much I know, and her father desperately needs money for some financial manipulations of his own."

He shuffled the papers together. "I never had a family, sir, and knew little of women. I was a lonely man, and she made me very comfortable before we were married, and I suddenly began to want a home.

"I am afraid I was very easy," he added, "and I now know her father led her to marry me hoping to get inside information on some of my activities. What they did not realize is that all my business I carry in my head. I never discuss business, and keep no records where they can be seen."

Returning to New York he had screened all his actions with care. He liquidated some more stocks, purchased several pieces of land, and bought suddenly and heavily in railroad shares. He deposited money where he would have access to it in case of need, and selected a name under which to receive mail if that should be necessary. Then he shipped to himself, at two different addresses, using this name, a box of books and two other cases of various articles he might require.

With the Baltimore attorney he arranged a code

name, a code for special dealings, and certain transfers of property. He also wrote checks closing his various accounts on specified days following his disappearance.

Announcing casually, as he often did, that he was going to Virginia for the shooting, he left New York.

As his wife had never wanted to go anywhere with him he was not surprised that she asked no questions. He had not told her that he knew of her plot to have him killed and, although they lived in the same house, they did not live together.

Neither she nor her father had any idea of the sort of man with whom they were dealing. The killing was planned to occur during a card game. The man hired was a Mississippi riverboat gambler who was promised his freedom on a plea of self-defense.

The gambler knew the story of the gunfight at The Crossing, but there was nothing to connect the youngster of that shooting with the immaculate New York financier.

The gambler received his first hint that all was not as he had expected during the early part of the game. Kettleman played shrewdly and with icy control, and the gambler quickly grasped that he himself was being studied with cool, calculated interest. As part of his scheme, the gambler deliberately invited an accusation of cheating whenever a showdown developed between Kettleman and himself, but Kettleman ignored the opportunity, and the gambler grew worried.

Nothing was going as planned, and he began to realize that his opponent knew what he was trying to do, and was deliberately avoiding it. So anxious was he to lead Kettleman into an argument that his mind was not on the game, and suddenly he lost a large pot.

Startled, he looked at the table and realized that he himself had been cheated, with coolness and effrontery. He had been stripped of more than six thousand dollars with the skill of a professional. His eyes lifted to Kettleman's.

"You have been looking for trouble," Kettleman said quietly. "I am offering it to you."

The gambler was nervous. He touched his tongue to his lips and felt the sweat beading his forehead.

"You are looking for trouble," Kettleman said. "Why?"

There was no one close by. "I am going to kill you," the gambler said.

"If you wish to leave the game, we can divide the pot, and I will forget what you have said."

It was there then—a way out. As a gambler he knew he should take it, but gambling was only a part of his business and he had his pride.

"I cannot. I have been paid."

"There are other ways to make a living and you have chosen the wrong one. I am offering you your last chance. Get out."

"I gave my word. I took their money."

Kettleman had seemed almost negligent. "When you are ready, then."

The gambler stepped back quickly, overturning his chair. "If you say I cheat," he said loudly, "you are a liar!" And he grasped his gun.

Everybody saw him grasp the gun, everybody saw him start to draw it, and then he started coughing and there was blood on his shirt, blood dribbling down his chin, and on his face the realization of death.

Kettleman leaned over him. He looked down at the gambler and knew this man was only a step away from the man he was himself. "I didn't want to kill you," he said. "Who hired you?"

"Your wife," the gambler said. "And her father."

Kettleman realized then that he had known something like this would happen. He started to rise but the gambler caught his wrist. "I must know. *Who are you?*"

Kettleman hesitated. For the first time since that night he spoke of it. "I was the kid at The Crossing."

"God!" The gambler was excited. He started to rise, began to speak, and then he died.

Kettleman turned away. "I saw it, sir." The speaker was a man powerful in the state government. "You had to do it."

Seeing an acquaintance, Kettleman said, "I am sorry for this. Will you see that he is buried well? I will pay."

At the estate in Virginia he wasted no time. He changed clothes, repacked his bags, and caught the ride with the peddler he knew would be coming through. He also knew it would be months before the peddler came that way again.

From a distant town he took a stage, and then a train.

By the time they discovered his absence, he would be safely in the hideout in New Mexico.

It was very cold. He sat up in his blankets and put fuel on the fire.

His thoughts returned to the girl on the train. She

had been singularly self-possessed, with a quiet beauty not easily forgotten.

Thinking of her made him remember his own wife, and he was amazed at how gullible he had been. His life had not fitted him for living with people. As a predatory creature he had been successful, as a human being he was a failure. He had invited no friendships and offered none.

He had entered business as he had life, to fight with fang and claw. Cool, ruthless, intelligent, he subordinated everything to success, and confided in no one, prepared to protect himself at all times, and to attack, always attack.

He had moved swiftly but with the sharp attention of a chess player, leaving nothing to chance. Nor had he ever attacked twice in the same way. He had developed an information service of office boys, messengers, waiters, cleaning women. They listened and reported to him, and he used the information.

It was a time of gamblers, a period of financial manipulation when fortunes were made and lost overnight. Mining, railroads and shipping, land speculation and industry—he had a hand in them all, shifting positions quickly, negotiating behind the scenes, working eighteen to twenty hours a day for days on end.

There had been periods of vague disquiet when the yearning within him reached out toward the warmth of others, but he fought down the impulse, stifling it. Occasionally, with subordinates or strangers, he had done some sudden, impulsive kindness, and was always ashamed of the lapse.

Of his early years he had only vague recollections. The one real thing in those years had been Flint.

That he had been found beside the burned-out wagon train, he knew. There were vague recollections of a woman crying, and of a man and woman who bickered and drank constantly. She had been kind to him when sober, maudlin when drinking, and there were times when she forgot all about him and he went hungry.

When he was four he heard the shot that destroyed the only world he knew. He had gone into the next room, rubbing the sleep from his eyes, to find the woman sprawled on the floor. He had often seen her like that, but this time there was blood on her back and side. Then people had come and taken him away.

After that he lived two years on a dry farm where there was little to eat and a losing battle was fought against big cattlemen. One day the farmers, fighting their own brutal struggle to survive, abandoned him on the street of a town.

He was sitting there at daybreak, shivering with the long night's chill, when a cold-eyed man in a buffalo coat rode into town, went past him, then turned back.

He remembered the cold, gray eyes, the unshaven jaw, and the questions the man asked. He had answered directly and simply, the only way he knew. The man had leaned down and lifted him to the saddle, and down the street in an all-night saloon and stage station, the man bought him a bowl of hot stew and crackers. He was sure he had never eaten anything that tasted so good. He had eaten, then fallen asleep.

When he awakened he was on the saddle in front

of the man. They rode for several days, always by the least-traveled trails.

The man took him to a house in a city and left him there with a woman. The next morning, Flint was gone.

The woman was kind, and she took him to a school where he was admitted. He remained there for eight years.

The studies were hard. The other students complained often. But for the first time he slept in a decent bed and had regular meals. He dreaded the day when he might have to leave, and somehow he got the idea that if he failed as a student he would be taken out of school.

When he was ten he made two discoveries at the same time, the first was the library, and the second was that the teachers at the school were curious about him. He found that by reading in the library he could anticipate lessons and find background for the essays the teachers constantly demanded. In this way he discovered the wonderful world of books.

The other students came from wealthy or well-to-do homes, but his tuition came from a variety of western towns. He was asked many probing questions, but replied to none of them.

During the long days of riding before they reached the house of the woman, Flint had taught him things that remained in his mind and, he now realized, had shaped his entire life.

"Never let them know how you feel or what you are thinking. If they know how you feel they know how to hurt you, and if they hurt you once, they will try again.

"Don't trust anybody, not even me. To trust is a weakness. It ain't necessarily that folks are bad, but they are weak or afraid. Be strong. Be your own man. Go your own way, but whatever you do, don't go crossways of other folks' beliefs.

"Keep your knowledge to yourself. Never offer information to anybody. Don't let people realize how much you know, and above all, study men. All your life there will be men who will try to keep you from getting where you're going, some out of hatred, some out of cussedness or inefficiency."

When the day came that the headmaster sent for him he fought down his panic. The headmaster was a severe, cold New England man. "We will be sorry to lose you," he said. "You have been an excellent student. As of now you have a better education than many of our business and political leaders. See that you use it." The headmaster paused briefly. "You came to us under peculiar circumstances, recommended by people whom we respect. We know nothing of your family."

For the boy there had been no vacations. When others went to their homes, he had stayed at school, sitting for days alone in the library, reading.

"I would continue to read, if I were you. Books are friends that will never fail you. You are going into a hard world. Remember this: honor is most important, that, and a good name. Keep your self-respect.

"You lack, I believe, an essential to happiness. You do not understand kindness." The headmaster shuffled papers on his desk. "I know that because I have never understood it myself, and it is a serious fault which I was long in appreciating. I hope it takes you less long."

From his desk the headmaster took an envelope. "This was enclosed in the letter which terminated your schooling."

Kettleman did not open the letter until he was alone. It was brief and to the point.

> *You was settin on the street when I seen you, and you was hungry. I fed you. Figgered a boy needed schoolin, so I sent you. Ever year I paid. You are old enough to make out. I got nothing more for you.*
> *Come to Abilene if you want.*
>
> > *Flint*

Five twenty-dollar bills were enclosed. He packed his clothes and, with nothing better to do, went to Abilene.

There was no one there named Flint.

After several days of inquiring he met a bartender who gave him a careful look and then suggested he stick around.

At school he had learned to ride, for it had been a school for young gentlemen. He got a job riding herd on some cattle, fattening for the market. It was not cowpunching, just keeping the cattle from drifting. The others were cowhands, however, so he learned a good deal.

After three months the cattle were sold. He went to work in a livery stable. He was there when Flint came.

The wind moaned in the pines. He replenished the fire, and lay back in his blankets again. The boughs bent above him, the fire crackled, and far off a horse's hooves drummed. The coals glowed red and pulsing. Looking up through the pines he could see a single star.

He could be no more than thirty miles from Flint's hideout in the malpais.

He awakened sharply, every sense alert. He heard a distant shout, and then a reply so close he jumped from his blankets.

"He can't be far! Search the trees!"

Swiftly he drew on his boots and swung the gun belt around his lean hips, then shrugged into the sheepskin. There was no time to eliminate signs of his presence here, so he simply faded back into the deeper shadows, taking the shotgun with him.

Brush crashed. A rider pushed through, then another.

"Hell! That ain't his fire! He had no time!"

"Somebody waitin' for him, maybe."

"Whoever it was"—the second rider's voice was sharp with command—"had no business on this range. Throw that bed on the fire."

Kettleman stepped from the shadows, the shotgun ready in his hands. "The blankets are mine." Without taking his eyes from the riders he threw a handful of brush on the fire, which blazed up. "And if he lays a hand on that bed, I'll blow you out of your saddle."

"Who the devil are you?" The older man's tone was harsh. "What are you doing here?"

"Minding my own business. See that you do the same."

"You're on my range. That makes your being here my business. Get off this range, and get off now."

"Like hell."

The man called Kettleman felt a hard, bitter joy mounting within him. So he was going to die. Why die in bed when he could go out with a gun in his hand? He could cheat them all now, and go as Flint had gone, in a blaze of gunfire.

"When you say this is your range, you lie in your teeth. This is railroad land, owned, deeded, and surveyed. Now understand this: I don't give a damn who you are, and I like it here. You can start shooting and I'll spread you all over that saddle."

He felt the shock of his words hitting them, and knew they were taken aback, as in their place he would have been, by his fury. The fact that he held a shotgun on them at less than twenty paces was an added factor.

"You're mighty sudden, friend." The man in command held himself carefully, aware that he faced real trouble, and sensing something irrational in the sharpness of the counter-attack. "Who are you?"

"I'm a man who likes his sleep, and you come hooting and hollering over the hills like a pack of crazy men. I take it you're hunting somebody, but with all that noise he's probably hidden so well you couldn't find him anyway. You act like a lot of brainless tenderfeet."

"That's hard talk, for a stranger."

"There's nothing strange about this shotgun. It can get almighty familiar."

"I've twenty men down below. What about them?"

"Only twenty? They make noise enough for eighty. Why, I'd have a half dozen of them down before they knew what they were up against, and the rest of them would quit as soon as they knew you weren't around to pay them for fighting."

A voice called through the trees. "Boss? Are you all right?"

"Tell them to go about their business," Kettleman said. "And then you do the same."

The rider turned his head. "Beat it, Sam. I'll be along in a minute. Everything is all right."

He turned back to Kettleman. "There's something here I don't understand. What are you doing here? What do you want?"

"Not a damned thing. Not a single damned thing."

The rider dismounted, then turned to his companion. "Bud, you ride along and help the others. I'll meet you at White Rock."

Bud hesitated. "It's all right, Bud, there will be no trouble with this man. Never tackle a man who doesn't care whether he lives or not. He will always have an edge on you."

He was short, with square shoulders, prematurely gray hair, and he wore a mustache. His hard, dark eyes studied Kettleman with care.

Obviously puzzled, he glanced around the camp, seeking some clue. His eyes found the big game rifle. "That's quite a weapon. Must be hard to get ammunition though."

"I load my own."

"I see." The rancher got out a cigar and lighted it. "A man with a rifle like that—well, if he was a good enough shot, he could make himself a lot of money."

Kettleman was bored. Daylight was not far-off and he badly needed rest. Talk of money irritated him, anyway. He could buy this rancher and give him away and never miss what it cost, and how much could it help him now?

"My name is Nugent. I'm a cattleman."

"All right."

Nugent was accustomed to respect and Kettleman's impatience angered him. Wind stirred the flames, and he added a few sticks. Poking at the fire gave him time to think. There had to be a reason for the man's presence. No cowhand could afford such weapons. The rifle alone must have cost several hundred dollars.

"You said something about this being railroad land."

Nugent was fishing now, and Kettleman smiled to himself. Experts had tried to get information from him. He shrugged. "At least half the land along any railroad right of way is railroad land, isn't it?"

Nugent was not satisfied. He had a suspicion the man was amused by him, and such a thought was unbearable. He treated Nugent like an inferior. Nugent was not accustomed to being so treated and did not like it. The flat-heeled boots did not go with cow country, and the man's clothing showed little wear.

"I never knew a man who did not want something."

"You are looking at one."

Nugent got to his feet and Kettleman arose, too. "I don't like a man who takes a crowd when he goes hunting."

Really angry, Nugent replied shortly, "Even the law does it."

"You are not the law. I think a man who can't do his own hunting is a coward."

Nugent's face went white, and with an effort he

fought down the urge to reach for a gun. But he was no gunfighter, and knew it.

"My advice to you is to clear out. We don't take to hard-talking strangers."

Deliberately, Kettleman yawned. "Get the hell out of here. I want to sleep."

Unable to think of a reply that might not get him killed, Nugent walked to his horse and mounted.

"I'll see you later," Nugent said when he was in the saddle. "If I didn't have a squatter to chase, I'd—"

"Squatter?" Kettleman smiled at him. "Why, you're only a squatter yourself. You don't own a foot of range. You came in here a few years ago and started running a few cattle on land that doesn't belong to you. Now of a sudden you are talking of squatters. You're a pompous little man with a bellyful of importance. Now get out of here."

Blind with fury, Nugent wheeled his horse and rode away, spurring the animal madly. By the Almighty! He would get his hands and come back, and . . .

Something went over him like a dash of ice-cold rain.

How did this stranger know all *that*? Who was he?

Kettleman rolled his bed swiftly, slung his haversack and blanket roll and, picking up his shotgun and rifle, he started along the ridge. It was still some time until daybreak, but if Nugent did come back he had no desire to be caught sleeping, and the rancher was mad enough to gather his crew and return.

Thomas S. Nugent. He knew the name from the files. Before building the railroad they had made a study of ranchers in the area to gauge the amount of shipping there would be to handle their cattle and what supplies they might require. There was not a ranch in the area about which he was uninformed. Because of the proximity to Flint's old hideout, he had paid particular attention to the vicinity.

It was faintly gray in the east when he climbed out of the hollow and started across country.

He was heavily loaded for the long walk that lay before him, but his illness seemed to have taken little toll of his strength as yet. He had always been strong, and even in New York he had been active, with regular workouts in the gym, a good bit of walking, and hunting trips to Virginia or over in New Jersey.

He had been walking only a short distance when he found the hunted man.

CHAPTER 2

NANCY KERRIGAN OPENED her eyes as the train slowed for a stop, and watched the stockyards flip past the windows like the spots on a riffled deck of cards. It was good to be home, despite the trouble she brought with her.

The straw-haired man was on his feet, and when he glanced back along the car she noticed the pockmarks on his cheeks and a tiny white scar above one eyebrow. He was very tall, and the way in which he flipped the gun belt around his hips spoke of long practice.

She had never seen this man before but she had lived too long in the West not to know his kind. Since the Lincoln County war and the Land-Grant fights there had been many of his kind in New Mexico, and now there were rumors of trouble building in the Tonto Basin of Arizona.

Yet this man was not going to the Basin. He was leaving the train at Alamitos.

She became aware that he was looking past her with sudden sharp attention. His eyes flickered over the car again, returning to the seats behind her, and involuntarily she turned to look. The man who had been seated back there was gone.

The train had made no stops, and this was the only passenger car. Yet the man was gone.

Obviously disturbed by something he did not understand, the big gunman's eyes rested briefly on her, and for an instant he seemed about to speak. The train slowed and steam drifted past the windows. She picked up her bag and walked down the aisle.

Conscious of being stared at, she glanced at a stocky man in a broadcloth suit and derby hat, his florid face and glassy blue eyes directed at her with singularly disagreeable attention. She averted her eyes, yet she had a feeling his interest was not entirely due to the fact that she was a woman.

When she descended to the platform Ed Flynn was waiting for her near the corner of the freight depot.

Nancy Kerrigan was a girl who found her home attractive. She had gone to school in the East, but for her the world revolved around Alamitos, the high plains of her own ranch, her cattle, the men who worked for her, and particularly, the wild, free country.

She had lived at Kaybar most of her life except for her time at school, and a few visits to friends, and for her it had always seemed the ultimate in security. Now that security was menaced in a way she had never believed would be possible. And with it, her whole future was at stake.

Ed Flynn took the bag from her hand and started toward the buckboard. Flynn had come west with her father and uncle, and had helped to found the Kaybar. Since her father's death he had been foreman. No businessman, he was nevertheless an excellent cattleman, understanding range conditions and the fattening of cattle as few men did.

She drew his attention to the straw-haired gunman. Flynn put her bag in the buckboard and then said quietly, "Whoever is paying the bills is going first class. That's Buckdun."

The name was legend. Buck Dunn, shortened by common usage to Buckdun, was known wherever range riders gathered. A professional fighting man, at times a bounty hunter, rarely a town-tamer, he was always a hunter and killer of men.

Nancy Kerrigan was familiar with cow-country gossip. Often enough the fighting in cattle or sheep wars was done by the hands on the job, without importing gunmen, and many a rancher was prepared to handle his own shooting chores. But when men like Buckdun came to town, somebody was preparing for war.

As Flynn helped Nancy into the buckboard she saw him glance across the street, and two Kaybar men sauntered from the walk in front of the store and got into their saddles. They were Pete Gaddis and Johnny Otero.

"Armed escort?"

Ed Flynn nodded grimly. "Two weeks has done a lot to this country."

"Has there been trouble?"

"Nugent lost fifty head of steers. He trailed them south along the malpais and then they just seemed to drop off the world."

"Rustlers?" Nancy was incredulous.

"When your father and I came into this country we didn't have a neighbor within a hundred miles in any direction, leaving out Indians, but this country is changing fast. Yes, there are rustlers working now. For the first time."

Nancy waved at Gaddis and Otero.

Johnny Otero had grown up on the Kaybar where

his father had been one of their first hands. He was New Mexican, his family coming up from Mexico more than a hundred years before. On his mother's side the family had been living around Santa Fe since before the Pilgrims landed at Plymouth Rock. Now nineteen, Johnny was considered the best rifle shot in the country.

Pete Gaddis had been at the ranch only four years, the newest of their hands with one exception, and he had a reputation for being a tough man, in any kind of a fight. Gaddis had been a shotgun guard on the Cheyenne to Deadwood stage, deputy marshal in a tough cowtown, and a warrior in more than one range war. A short, solidly built man, he was a top hand.

Flynn struck a match with his left hand and cupped it in his left palm to his cigar. "Burris and two strangers filed a homestead on a piece of Nugent's range, claiming it was government land and open for filing," he said. "You know Tom Nugent. He flew off the handle and burned them out and there was a shooting. The homesteaders showed fight and shot a Nugent rider out of the saddle. One of the strangers died right there and the last I heard Nugent and his crowd were hunting the other one off east of here."

"What happened to Burris?"

"He lit out for Alamitos like his tail was afire, and they let him go."

Nancy Kerrigan started to explain the situation to Flynn, then decided to wait until she had thought it out and decided upon a course. Ed Flynn was good at handling men and cattle, but had little imagination and was hesitant to offer advice. The business side of the ranch she had been handling even before her father died. Besides, the decision must be her own, as Kaybar was her own.

"Do you think," she asked suddenly, "that Port Baldwin had anything to do with those squatters?"

Flynn was astonished. He flicked the ash from his cigar against the whipstock. "I never gave it any thought," he said honestly. "You take after the colonel, Nancy, you surely do. That sounds like the colonel himself."

Alone in her room, Nancy took the pins from her hat and removed it, fluffing her hair a little, and thinking about the results of her trip to Santa Fe.

Outside on a far green slope cattle fed, and just over that low hill the streams all flowed toward the Pacific Ocean, while here, where the ranch was situated, they flowed toward the Atlantic. The low hill out there was the Continental Divide, although it could not be guessed from a casual glance.

Supposedly her trip to Santa Fe had been like all the others, to shop for new clothes or things for the ranch. She had shopped, but her major purpose had been to consult her father's lawyer.

To Nancy, the Kaybar was one of the few permanent things in a changing world until she overheard a casual comment in the store in Alamitos one day while getting her mail.

A couple of drummers waiting to see the proprietor had been discussing land titles and their general insecurity.

The idea nagged at her consciousness until she went to her father's desk and the big iron safe and got out the ranch papers. There were bills, receipts, records of cattle bought or sold, payroll records, and lists of expenditures and planned development, but there was no deed.

Everything had been kept with meticulous care, and had there been a deed it would have been among those papers.

When her father and uncle had come west title deeds had no importance. They stopped where there was water and grass and they "owned" land by right of possession. That right was never questioned in the early days except by roving Indians. Colonel Kerrigan had talked business with the Indians and had bought land from them. Several times since then he had, when the years were bad and the Indians hungry, given them a few head of steers.

For a long time there had been nobody else within miles, the ranch had grown larger, the few deals made had been by driving cattle east, selling to the Army or to survey parties.

It had taken the trip to Santa Fe to show Nancy how flimsy was this rock upon which she was building her life.

Her father and uncle had settled on the land eighteen years before when she was scarcely three, and she had come to live on Kaybar when she was five. Twice, before she left for school, she had survived Indian attacks on the ranch, both by roving bands of Paiutes.

They had a claim, the judge assured her, by right of possession, and such claims were usually allowed, but settlers were streaming west and Congress was looking favorably on the claims of the settlers wanting land. That her father had bought land from the Indians might not help at all, for another Indian could always be found to dispute the right of the original Indians to sell land at all.

Out on the knoll west of the ranch house, and not quite to the Continental Divide, were buried her father, her aunt and uncle, and three cowhands who had died in fights to save the ranch from Indians. Buried in a neat row along the farther fence of the little cemetery were nine Paiutes and three White Mountain Apaches who had died trying to massacre the ranchers.

Nancy got out the carefully drawn map her father had prepared of the range where their cattle grazed. The ranch lay south of the railroad and, roughly, from the Divide to the lava beds, called the malpais, and south to the Datil Mountains. What was called the home ranch, however, comprised fifty-five sections of land. With the exception of a few widely scattered meadows used to grow hay against the winter, none of it could be considered farm land.

For a long time she studied the map. It was a good map, for her father had been an Army engineer in the war with Mexico, and had had good training in the field. Every waterhole was carefully marked as well as seeps and such places where water might be found in the wet years. Upon those waterholes the ranch depended; without them the ranchers could not exist, nor could anyone else.

Cattle would walk miles for water, but there was a point beyond which it would not pay for they walked off good beef. That was why several of the waterholes on the range had been developed by themselves, maintained by themselves, to keep the stock from wandering farther than necessary.

From earliest childhood she had been taught to accept responsibility, and to make her own decisions and abide by them. "Every youngster wants to be grown-up," her father had said, "but the difference between a child and an adult is not years, rather it's a willingness to accept responsibility, to be responsible for one's own actions."

It was a lesson she learned well, and in the years since the death of her father the ranch under her management had earned money and improved in value. It was she who had conceived the idea of digging for water and thus creating new waterholes.

Nancy went to the door. Flynn was standing near the corral, talking to Pete Gaddis.

"Ed, will you come here a minute? And don't go away, Pete. I want to talk to you, too."

When Flynn was seated she had Juana, the Mexican girl, bring coffee. Then she explained why she had gone to Santa Fe. He sat very still, not looking at her, but tracing imaginary patterns on the table with his finger.

"Ed," she said finally, "we shall have to move fast. I have a bad feeling about all this. I want you to file on Iron Springs. I'd like Pete Gaddis to file on the Blue Hole, and Johnny Otero on Rock House. The ranch will provide everything needed and when the land has been proved up, we will buy it from you."

"How will we manage it? If we all start a run on Santa Fe, somebody will start asking questions."

"You'll go by yourself. I want you to ride to Horse Springs, Ed, and take the stage from there. Come back the same way. I'd like it if nobody knew you were gone."

He glanced up quickly. Ed Flynn did not know whether Nancy Kerrigan knew about Gladys Soper or not. Nancy was, Ed often thought, a very uncertain girl sometimes. Maybe she knew that he had been keeping Gladys and maybe she did not. Of one thing he was sure; Nancy Kerrigan would never admit it if she did.

"Nobody" meant Gladys, too. And that could make a difficulty.

"It will have to be you, Ed," Nancy was saying. "They know you and they will file for you without creating any talk. And that is the way I want it."

Gladys had plans for the next few days. This trip would raise hob with those plans, and Gladys could be difficult when she wished. Damn it, if there was only some way ...

"And, Ed. Let's double the saddle stock we're keeping up. We'll be doing a lot of riding from now on."

It was the coming of the railroad that changed everything, Nancy thought. True, they had made a lot of money supplying beef to the workers when the road was being built but, when the railroad went in, the riffraff came.

That man on the train, with the florid face and the pale-blue eyes, now. Who was he? Why was he here? And why had he tried to attract her attention?

Had he known who she was? Had he guessed why she was in Santa Fe?

CHAPTER 3

KETTLEMAN PAUSED ABRUPTLY upon seeing the man sprawled in the brush. Standing close against the trunk of a pine, Kettleman surveyed the area with extreme care. Only when he was positive that he was alone did he approach the fallen man.

He lay on a gentle slope and, for concealment, he could not have fallen in a better position. Approached from any other angle he would have been invisible.

Kettleman knelt and examined the man. He was not dead. His pulse was strong. He had lost blood, but from a quick examination, Kettleman could find only a flesh wound. A bullet had cut through the heavy muscle under his arm.

Gathering a few sticks of curl leaf and dry cedar, Kettleman built a small, smokeless fire and when he had heated some water, he bathed the wound. As he worked the man moaned, then opened his eyes and stared at Kettleman.

"Who are you?"

"That's what Nugent asked me. And you'd better be getting out of here because he will be coming back this way."

With an effort the man sat up. "Can you carry double? I got to hide. Nugent figures to kill me."

"Sorry . . . I have no horse." Kettleman gathered his

gear and stowed it. "And don't ask further help from me because you know this country better than I do."

"You ain't much help." The wounded man stared at him sourly. "What am I going to do?"

"Your problem. But I'd begin by getting out of here, because I do think Nugent intends to kill you, and I don't blame him. You aren't much good."

The wounded man's face flushed angrily. "What the hell do you know?"

"I know I cleaned your wound and you didn't even take time to thank me." Kettleman slung his packs again and picked up his weapons. "Whoever hired you had to go pretty far to find a man."

"Who said anybody hired me?" The man's eyes were cunning.

"Your kind is always hired," Kettleman replied, "and seldom worth the cost. You're on your own."

He turned sharply into the brush, not wanting his back to the man, then changed course and went into the deepest part, moving softly as possible. Turning west again he passed the ruins of an old pueblo, and paused to study his back trail. There was no sign of movement. Then he examined the country around him, and chose the best route toward the lava beds. He wanted to keep off the horizon, not being eager to reply to inquiries nor to encounter any of Nugent's men.

An hour later, from the crest of a ridge he could see far and away the smoke of a train. The air was very clear and fresh, and he breathed deeply. Off to the north he could see two mesas lifting their square rock shoulders against the sky. One of them was topped by buildings and a thread of smoke went up from them. That would be Acoma, the sky city.

The sky was very blue, here and there a fluff of white cloud. It was a lovely country, and too bad he had so little time left to enjoy it.

For the first time he felt a sharp twinge of regret, and he walked on with long, swinging strides. It would not do to find things to love at this late date, even so fair a land. Inside him this thing was growing, slowly capturing his life, and it was better that he go remembering nothing that he wanted to remember.

There was a place on the edge of Ceboletta Mesa that he had to find, where the mesa sent a rocky shoulder toward the lava beds. That point was the key to the opening he was looking for.

Several times he sat down to rest, although he did not like to sit down, and had never been one to delay short of a goal. Yet his strength was waning and his legs were growing very tired. The walking here was nothing like the walking he had done behind hunting dogs in Virginia or New Jersey. This was rough and rocky, and he had climbed nearly three thousand feet since leaving the railroad.

Skirting the edge of a wooded area he crossed a plateau dotted with small lakes and emerged within fifty yards of the point he had been seeking. Before him, and some distance lower down, lay the lava beds, the dreaded malpais.

Like a fat, enormous snake it lay stretched across the country, a black and ugly mass of twisted, rope-like rock, clinkers and piles of lava, that looked like hell with the fires out, filling its sterile sink and winding south and north for many miles.

This was desolation. This was what remained after Mount Taylor and El Tintero spewed forth their flaming rock and drenched the country with liquid fire so that the Indians fled the country in terror and were long in returning.

The river of lava had flowed southward, killing everything in its path, flattening stone houses or flowing through them, flowing downhill, piling up to cross over hills, falling in cascades down steep cliffs, until finally it solidified into a great stream of natural glass, leaving behind all the formations lava can create. Hardening from the outside, often the lava continued to flow beneath the surface and left vast caverns, roofed over in places by blisters of apparently solid rock that was actually eggshell thin.

Splitting at places into separate streams it left islands of grass like sunken parks, dotted with trees and surrounded by walls of lava sometimes fifty feet high. Underneath were perpetual ice caves.

It was in one of these islands of green, Kettleman knew, that Flint had found his hideout.

No tracks or other evidence of travel lay in the bottom of the narrow crack Flint had followed to the hidden oasis. So narrow throughout most of its length that a horseman's feet brushed the lava walls on either side, it was at no place wider than a tall man's outstretched arms could reach.

It wound, twisted, bent sharply and seemed to end a dozen time before reaching a rock-walled acre of grass and trees. Against the wall, Flint had built a rock house, using the building blocks provided by the lava flow itself. Adjoining the rock house he built a wall, closing off a cave mouth to be used as a stable. By facing an undercut cliff with stone, he had constructed a passage from the cabin to the stable so he could move from one to the other in perfect shelter.

The cave itself was a long tunnel that led through two hundred yards of rock to a much larger island of grass and trees where a small stream flowed. In this place Flint had released several horses. One a stallion, three mares.

The entrance to the crack that led to this hideout was extremely difficult to find and Flint had discovered it purely by accident. The opening was masked by an overlapping wall of rock, invisible from even a few feet away.

Seated by the trunk of a cedar, Kettleman shed his pack and got out his glasses. The sun was far down in the west, and shadows had gathered in the hollows and cracks of the malpais. With infinite care Kettleman began to study the terrain below him.

Far away across the lava beds, perhaps six or seven miles distant, he could see an island of green. Otherwise what lay below him was a nightmare of desolation and death, and he could see no other oasis, no such place as Flint had mentioned.

Turning north he worked his way, his pack once more riding his chafed and aching shoulders, along the edge of the cliff. A path would be here, a narrow lip of a path negotiated by deer, antelope, and bear, occasionally by half-wild cattle.

The sun would soon be gone. It was unlikely that he would find the crack in the wall tonight. Several times he stopped, twisted by the pain in his stomach.

When he found the path he looked upon it with awe. Flint had said a good mountain horse could manage it, but if he did the rider's foot would hang over space.

Below all was blackness. Farther out the dying sun had turned the lava beds into a red flaming mass that relived for an instant in the sunset their former molten terror. Beyond the lava, miles away, a dark bulking shoulder of rock might be El Morro, the Inscription Rock, where, more than two hundred and fifty years before, Spanish men had signed their names.

Although the cliff down which he made his way lay deep in shadow the path could be clearly seen, and the lava beds were still bathed in slowly dulling red fire.

At the bottom the path ended in a maze of boulders and rocky debris outgrown with low brush and a few stunted trees. Once he barked his shins on the edge of a rock, and again he stumbled and fell to his knees. Finally he sat down and slid the pack from his back. He was exhausted.

Kettleman had never known weakness in his life, and never illness. His physical strength was enormous and he had learned to rely upon it, and now for the first time he was feeling weakness. He had walked a long way, driven on as much by determination to get where he was going as anything.

He sat very still, breathing hoarsely. He felt sick at his stomach and was afraid he was going to have more of those agonizing pains.

The shadows grew darker and the light faded from the lava beds. Only the sky remained a deeper blue, and here and there a bright star hung against the sky like a lamp. Still he did not move. His breathing eased, and the pains did not come, yet still he waited.

It was too late to find the crack in the rock now, and it might take him days, even with the landmarks Flint had provided. It was odd, how all through the years he had kept this place in mind as if he had known that some day he would come here.

He had no faith in people. He had avoided all close contacts with them when possible. Occasionally he had tricked himself into little kindnesses from some deep inner instinct or perhaps some vague desire for warmth and friendship. But he had brusquely rejected all thanks, and fled from appreciation.

He had never hated his wife or her father for what they had planned to do, nor for the times they had tried to profit by the connection. He did not hate them, for he had been taught to expect nothing better, and they were acting as he expected people to act.

From the day of his arrival in the East he had known but one ambition, and that was for wealth and power. He fought as Flint had taught him to fight, but using the weapons of his knowledge gained at school, his reading since that time, and the information acquired from day to day. He acted coldly, ruthlessly, yet shrewdly.

Kettleman's first job in the East was driving a hansom cab and he had deliberately sought it, as a way to learn the town, to see where the various types of people gathered, and to learn where the money was.

He overheard a discussion between two businessmen of a building they planned to put up and the way they intended to acquire the property for it. He moved in quickly the next morning at daybreak, bought an option on a key lot, and sold it two weeks later for a substantial profit.

Then he found a job as messenger for a brokerage house where he worked for a year, keeping his mouth shut and his eyes and ears open. He carefully kept his stake intact, and from time to time made small investments from it. A year after his arrival in New York he had tripled his original stake.

Each investment had been based upon information obtained during his working hours, and he never forgot how much a pair of attentive ears can overhear. Later, when he was in a position to do so, he deliberately hired such men to listen for him. Businessmen often discussed their affairs as though the driver of the hansom was deaf, and the information was often of value.

He was startled from his dreaming by the click of a hoof on stone, and he turned his head to see a rider coming down the trail along the lava beds. Behind him were strung out a bunch of cattle. Well concealed, Kettleman had only to sit still and allow them to pass. Three more riders brought up the rear, and he did not need to be told why the cattle were being moved at such an hour.

The last of the riders trailed some distance behind, and when he was almost up to Kettleman, he drew up.

It was completely dark now. Kettleman knew the rider had come to a halt because of the cessation of movement, and then he heard a creak of saddle leather as the man moved slightly in the saddle.

Kettleman made no move except to turn the shotgun toward the sound.

He heard a match strike and through the leaves he could see the light reveal momentarily, not a face as would be expected, but a hand. The rider had held the fire away from him, expecting to draw a shot.

Kettleman was amused, but he did not move. The match was dropped, and then another one lighted. "Well"—the voice was a soft drawl—"don't reckon you plan to shoot me, so why don't we talk?"

The horse stomped restlessly, but the man called Kettleman made no move. The unseen rider drew a cigarette down to the match, bending his head to meet his cupped hand, rather than otherwise. Kettleman caught a brief glimpse of a gaunt, hard-boned face, and then the match was blown out and there was only the glow from the cigarette.

"This horse," the soft drawl continued, "is a good night horse. Broke him from a wild bunch, and he's worth his weight in gold to a night-riding man. He spotted you first off. If you'd been a horse he would have whinnied, if you'd been a cow-critter he would have cut out after you, and he'd shy from a bear or a lion, so you've got to be a man."

The rider paused. "Something different about you, too. I can tell that by his attitude."

Kettleman remained still, curious to see what the rider would do next. And when the rider did speak his voice was plaintive. "Now, see here. I done my part. It's up to you. How's folks to get acquainted if somebody is so standoffish? If you're afraid of crowds, you needn't be. That bunch up ahead are gone to hell and gone by now. They sure are skittish.

"Why, I mind a time down in Texas—Say, who are you, anyhow?"

Kettleman decided the man's sharpness deserved its reward. It took a man with acute senses to detect from the actions of a ridden horse that he was not alone, and in the dark, at that.

"I am a man who minds his own affairs," he said aloud, "and that's all I ask of others."

"Talks mighty well, he does. Talks like a man who'd had schoolin', and I'd say there ain't too many of that kind around this neck of the hills.

"You might," the rider said suddenly, "jump the wrong fence and figure me for a rustler. As a matter of fact, I have rustled a few head, time to time, but that was in another country and a long time back.

"In spite of how it looked, I wasn't with those boys. Not in the rustling. You see, I know them, and I could figure that where they were, rustling would be, so I thought I'd ride out tonight and read them from the Book.

"You know, sort of set up an understandin', like. They do as they might, as long as they lay off the outfit I ride for. If they jump my brand, I told them I'd come huntin'."

The stub of the cigarette described a brief arc and hit against the lava, then lost itself in the rocks.

"Mighty one-sided, this here conversation," the rider said, "but if you happen to be one of those travelin' gunslingers who are riding into this country, you lay off the Kaybar. We don't want any trouble."

"Neither do I," Kettleman said, "and we're not likely to run into each other again."

There was a silence for a minute or two, but the rider showed no disposition to move on. Kettleman could almost sense the man's curiosity. Finally, the rider said, "Now there's a strange thing. You say I'll not see you again—run into you, I mean. This is a big country, but not so big that folks can miss each other very easy. I'm going to be around. What's going to happen to you that I won't see you?"

When there was no reply, the rider said, "This is a good country, friend." He paused, and then he added, "If you're on the dodge you might like to know there isn't even a town marshal in Alamitos—never needed one.

"Folks ain't inclined to pry, although there's newcomers around. Some of them are building up to be mighty unpopular."

"I know nothing about things here," Kettleman replied, "and I have no interest in local affairs."

He found himself liking the cool, quiet-talking man. He heard a whisper of paper and knew the man was building another cigarette.

"You're not from hereabouts, or I'd recall your voice," the rider said, "and I know almost everybody around. You don't fit anywhere unless you're a friend of Port Baldwin."

Kettleman felt a cool wind blowing down the canyon. He waited, and then he said, "I don't know the man. Does he live here?"

"Newcomer. From back East somewhere. He just moved into the country with forty thousand head of cows and that means he's got to crowd everybody off their range. I think he knew that when he came in."

Porter Baldwin. He had never met him but he knew his name. It was one of those things he believed he had left behind.

"Is he the one who is importing the gunfighters?"

"That's the one. Although Tom Nugent may do the same."

"And what about your outfit?"

"Kaybar?" The man chuckled. "I suppose the boys over there would say I was the gunfighter for Kaybar. I'd not claim the job for myself but they might claim it for me. And there's a salty bunch at Kaybar. The colonel knew how to pick them."

"Knew?"

"He's dead. His daughter handles the outfit."

"How does a girl figure to lead a war?"

"If a girl can do it, this one can. She's a girl to ride the river with, I'd say. I'd not want a better boss."

The rider was silent for a few minutes, then said, "I'm going to ride along." He paused. "You got grub? coffee?"

"Thanks. I do have them."

"But no horse. And that's a curious thing. A man afoot in this country isn't going far."

The rider turned his mount. "If you want to look me up, you ask for Pete Gaddis."

Kettleman listened to the sound of the retreating horse, strangely drawn to the man who had talked so quietly into the night. Gaddis had wanted to talk, and to a stranger.

So. Porter Baldwin.

The past then was not so far behind. Yet Baldwin could have no idea that Kettleman was anywhere around. So what was Baldwin planning? Why had Baldwin suddenly come into this area with forty thousand head of cattle? Baldwin knew nothing of cattle and wasn't likely to get interested in them.

His mind, long attuned to business combat, now began to seek out causes and effects, searching for the hidden motivations behind Baldwin's move. Gaddis had said, "That means he's got to crowd somebody off their range." That must be it.

The interest then was not cattle, but land. Land here was held by big cattle outfits, the government, or the railroad. And Baldwin had done no negotiating with the railroad.

The moon was rising, and he had not considered the moon. Living in cities, a man rarely looked at the sky.

He shouldered his pack, hung the rifle from his shoulder by its sling and, carrying the shotgun, he started out. When he was opposite the point of rock he crossed the dry watercourse and bedded down among the rocks. During the night he was awakened by pain. The pain twisted his vitals and he grew weak and sick and it was a long time before it passed off, and he slept.

When he awakened again he was weak and drenched with cold sweat. He got up and built a small fire and huddled over it, shivering and chilled. The moonlight lay weirdly upon the ghostly rocks and threw eerie shadows along the sandy way where the water had gone. Off to the east the wall of the mesa lifted, towering black against the sky, and dawn came slowly from a cold sky, and he did not make coffee or eat.

The gnawing pain in his stomach stayed with him, but he got up and shouldered his pack.

He could not be far from the entrance to the hideout. The wall of lava was about fifty feet high along here, huge black blocks of it, and then in places great wrinkled bulges like the skin of a sleeping elephant. He walked along a few steps, stepping from rock to rock where possible and holding close to the wall for fear of missing the entrance.

There was a lot of brush, stiff, wiry, and filled with thorns, clumps of prickly pear, and a few scattered pines. He had gone only a hundred yards or so when he felt a sickness in his stomach and he paused and leaned against the rock.

He was frightened.

The last thing he wanted was to die here, where he could be found. He must disappear, vanish completely. He waited, leaning against the rock. Finally he started on again. Only now his mind was made up. If he felt himself going he would use the last of his strength to crawl out on the lava bed. It would be a long time before they found him there.

The man called Kettleman crawled down through the rocks, and lowered himself into a hollow space where water had spilled over some boulders after heavy rains, then climbed up the bank. He had gone only a mile when he looked up at the wall opposite. There was a slash of white quartz there. Somehow he had missed the opening. How he could have done so he could not imagine, but miss it he had. Turning, he retraced his steps.

Twice he rested. It was almost noon before he found it. There was no brush concealing the opening, there was no jumble of boulders right at that point. The wall of lava took a slight bend, but in the open, where there was no evidence of any kind of an entrance. Kettleman had passed the place three times, thinking he had seen everything.

The lava was cracked and split in many places, and right before him there was such a split, a crack that seemed no more than three inches wide.

Yet when he stepped back he caught a glimpse out

of the corner of his eye of what appeared to be an optical illusion. He looked again. There was something wrong with the perspective in that crack. He walked slowly toward it, and when he was right up to the rock, he saw what it was. The left edge stood out almost four feet from the other side, and there was an opening that ran back into the rock parallel to the face. It seemed to go no more than six or seven feet and end in a blank wall. Yet when he stepped inside he saw that it wound back into the lava.

Turning, he went back to the edge of the opening and, standing there, he carefully surveyed the lip of the cliff opposite. For a long time he stayed there, letting his eyes rove along that lip. Only then did he move out from the rock and carefully brush away the few tracks he had made.

Returning to the opening in the wall he paused again to scan the rim of the cliff, but there was no sign of movement.

He walked into the narrow, winding crack, which steadily grew narrower and dipped down deeper and deeper. It was wide enough for a horse if the stirrups were tied up, and the overhang would prevent its being seen from above, should anyone venture out upon the lava, an extremely remote chance.

No man would venture upon the lava. Deer had been driven there by wolves, but their feet and legs became so badly lacerated they could not walk farther, and they died there.

It took him almost an hour to reach the hideout in the lava beds, and when he arrived, he stopped, deeply stirred by the beauty of the little oasis. The sides rose steeply and curved inward at the top. The area at the bottom was scarcely an acre in extent, but a small stream ran from under the rock on one side, meandered across and lost itself under the lava again.

There were several fruit trees, planted by Flint, and a patch of *chia,* whose seed was used as food by the Indians. Until he had looked for several minutes he did not see the cabin, for it was merely the walled-up face of a rocky overhang, the entrance shadowed by a cottonwood.

He walked slowly across the open grass toward a slit in the rock wall that apparently served as a window. He went past it and he found the door. It was a slab door, thick and strong. The man called Kettleman unlatched it and stepped inside.

The room was larger than he expected, with two bunks built against the far wall. There was a table, two chairs, hooks on the wall, and a bench with a washbasin. There was a trickle of running water from the spring, and from both the door and the window the opening into the basin could be seen, and the entire basin covered.

There was a broom.

He dusted off the bed, then dumped his own gear on it. Carefully, he swept, then built a small fire and made tea. When he had his tea and some hot broth he went to the door and sat down on the stoop, looking out over the hollow.

This was the place. It was here he was going to die.

CHAPTER 4

THE MAN CALLED Kettleman sat on the step of the rock house and looked out over the shadowing acres of green. He listened to the wind in the pines, and smelled the freshness of the high, cool air. Something stirred deep within him, something forgotten.

He had followed the lone trails, the ancient trails, the silent and mysterious trails with Flint. Wherever that strange and silent man wished to go, he seemed to know a hidden way to travel. For days on end they had ridden without speaking, their campfires surrounded by a vast and empty stillness.

He remembered the pungent smell of cedar, the smokiness of damp wood, the crisp crackle of pine, the deep red glow of dying fires, the sound of wind in the mesquite. How many fires had he fed with wood or buffalo chips? He had traveled the far rim of civilization, moving like a ghost across lands known only to roaming Indians.

Three years. Never once had Flint told him what they were about. Always he was left far behind to care for their horses and wait. Suddenly then, Flint would ride up and they would shift saddles and be gone again.

For Flint never directed his steps toward the saloons and gambling houses. After the jobs he did they would ride away into the wildest, most remote country, and then, sometimes, Flint would talk for long hours of the desert, the mountains, of how to survive under all conditions and how to live.

Kettleman got slowly to his feet and walked down to the water. He stood there, watching it chuckling over the stones. The gnawing in his stomach was always there now. There was but little time left.

Yet already some of the quietness of this place was seeping into him. The tension was going out of him, his muscles were mysteriously relaxing.

It was long after the stars came out before he slept, and then for a time he was dreamless, but he awakened, and sat up in the chill night and lighted his pipe. He walked to the door, and the air felt strangely damp, the stars very clear. He listened into the night, but heard no sound.

That girl on the train. He remembered the clear, honest way she had looked at him, the grace of her movements. Why had he not met such a girl when he was still alive?

For now he would die, like a wolf as he had lived, a lone wolf, in a dark place, snapping at his wounds. He had lived with bared teeth, and it was proper that he die that way.

That Gaddis now, Kettleman reflected. He liked the fellow. He had a slow, easy, half-amused way of talking that Kettleman liked.

There was a fight building. The straw-haired man on the train—a warrior if he had ever seen one.

And suddenly then he thought of Porter Baldwin.

A shrewd, tough, dangerous man. A promoter. Hardly a western man, but one who never moved without a purpose, and one with considerable experience in the knock-down and drag-out world of finance. He had been a blockade runner during the Civil War, running cotton and rifles through to the Confederate side, and selling information to the North.

He had been involved in the efforts to corner the gold market that Jim Fisk and Jay Gould had supposedly started.

If Porter Baldwin was out here, it was not because of cattle. There was money in cattle and they might be a side line for Baldwin, but he would not involve himself personally unless there was more behind it than the profits from cattle.

Well, it was no business of his. He knocked the ashes from his pipe, and went inside. When he awakened the sun was high, and it was the first good night's sleep he had had in a long time.

The gnawing pain was in his stomach, so he got out of bed and prepared a light breakfast. He moved slowly, taking his time about everything. As he ate, he planned his day. He must first of all find the passage to the inner island of grass. It was doubtful that, after these years, any horses remained, though they had been fine stock, young and in good shape and, Flint had assured him, there was feed for a dozen head and a water supply fed by the same stream that flowed through this oasis.

The few articles of food he had brought with him were scarcely sufficient for three days of sparse living, so he must go after supplies, and he wanted to pick up a box of books he had shipped to himself at Horse Springs.

Two other cases of books and supplies he had

shipped to Alamitos, not wanting to attract attention by appearing in either place too often, but he would need pack animals to get the stuff back here. However there was no hurry about anything but grub, and he wanted to get enough to last.

Flint had left the horses, a stallion and two or three mares, in the inner and larger basin. If they were alive they would be sixteen or seventeen years old. But there might be young stuff. The way to the basin lay through one of the long lava tunnels with which this place was riddled.

He walked down the passage Flint had made to join the cabin to the stable. He had simply taken slabs of rock without mortar and walled in an overhang of the cliff. In the back of the stable there was a manger built against the wall, a dark alcove behind it. Going into that stall he laid hold of the manger. It swung out on concealed hinges and he stepped back into the alcove and swung the manger into place behind him. The tunnel was there before him.

A shelf, head-high was on the right.

He put his hand up and found a few candles. He lighted one of them and walked into the passage. The height was uniform, not over eight feet, and the tunnel was for the greater distance about twice that in width. He counted nearly a hundred steps before he saw light.

He walked out into a little park.

There were perhaps three hundred acres of good grass here. Along the far side there were a dozen cottonwoods and some willows, and there were scattered pines.

Standing at the mouth of the lava conduit, he

counted seven horses, heads up, staring at him. He took three steps into the open so they could see him plainly.

One horse, a big bay standing at least seventeen hands, threw his head up sharply and blew loudly. He trotted forward a few steps, then pawed the ground.

"Want to fight, do you?" Kettleman talked softly to the horse. "I'm friendly, old man. Don't hunt trouble from me."

His eyes went to the other horses. Young stock—a couple of three- or four-year-olds, and a couple that were not such young stock. There was another horse, a mare, that was considerably older.

Flint had been a quiet man with horses, but he made pets of them all. Kettleman called them, the long, crooning call that Flint had used.

The old mare's head came around sharply. Did she remember? Did she remember enough?

Some said a horse did not remember for long, yet others claimed the opposite. He called again, and walked a few steps farther, holding out a piece of sugar as Flint always had.

Several of the horses began to walk away, the red stallion standing guard, head up, nostrils flared. The old mare stared at him. Tentatively, she came a step or two nearer, stretching out her nose as if to sniff.

He stood still, liking the warmth on his back. The sun was bright, a bee was droning among the brush near the wall of the park. He called again and went another step. The stallion shied, trotted a few steps to one side, then wheeled and trotted back. The mare stood her ground.

Yet she was nervous, and he did not want to

frighten her. He waited awhile longer and then went toward her. Just as she was about to shy away, he tossed the sugar toward her. She flipped her head, but moved off only a few steps, and when he left, she came up and sniffed the grass to see what he had thrown. He saw her nibbling at the sugar, but he did not go back.

The day was early and he had brought a book. He sat on a flat rock with the sun on him and read. The stallion circled nervously for a time, and then went to feeding as had the others.

After an hour he put the book aside and studied the layout of the big pasture.

It was a near perfect oval, with lava walls fifty to sixty feet high. There was a permanent water source from the same spring that provided water for the cabin. It flowed under the lava and into this park, but Flint had told him there was another water hole on the far side.

He was still tired from his walk of the previous day, and his leg muscles were stiff. There were few places a man might climb out of the oval, but nowhere a horse could escape. He was certain he was the only man these horses had seen, with the exception of the mare.

He spent most of the afternoon wandering about close to the tunnel mouth or reading, and then he retreated through the tunnel to the cabin and made some beef broth. Kettleman ate it slowly.

A few days more . . .

———

PETE GADDIS LEANED on the mahogany of the Divide Saloon. It was early evening and he had been in town only a few minutes. There were a lot of strangers around, most of them riders for the Port Baldwin outfit.

Red Dolan, the bartender, came toward Gaddis and put his big, thick-palmed hands on the edge of the bar. The two were friends. Neither had known the other before coming to Alamitos but what lay behind them was much the same.

"Not like the ones we used to know," Dolan commented, his eyes on the Baldwin riders. "Tough kids. Not like McKinney, or Courtright." Dolan took the cigar from his teeth. "Did you know Long-Haired Jim?"

Gaddis grunted. "Rode through Lake Valley, one time. He was around."

"Fast man. There were some good ones came out of Illinois. Courtright, Hickok—I could name a dozen."

"Knew a man served with Hickok in the Army. He was a good man then, too. He used to laugh at the stories told about him—killing eight or nine of the McCandless gang."

"They like to think we're wild and bloody out here, those folks back East do. Why, that Nichols lied in his teeth, and knew it. Hickok was in a bad way, just gettin' over a bear-scratching. He was in no shape for a fight then, and said so a dozen times. All the fighting he did on that day was with a gun."

Gaddis took a gulp of rye whiskey. "Buckdun's in town," he commented.

"That means somebody's going to die." Dolan relighted his cigar that had gone out. "But you're wrong. He's not in town. He rode out before day-break."

Gaddis considered the information. It seemed un-likely there was any connection, but Ed Flynn had ridden out before daybreak, too. Ed was bound south for Horse Springs, and nobody would know about that. Yet the more he thought of it, the more he wor-ried. Flynn was a good man—steady. But he was no match for Buckdun, even if Buckdun gave him a chance, which he wouldn't.

"Odd breed," Gaddis said. "I never could see dry-gulching a man."

Red Dolan's thoughts moved back down the years. "Yes," he mused, "they are an odd breed. I knew one, a long time ago. To him it was like fighting a war in which he was a soldier. Only I think he changed his mind about it, after awhile."

"What became of him?"

Dolan brushed the ash from his cigar. "Dropped off the end of the world. I never knew what happened to him—and I would have known."

"Friend?"

"Folks used to leave word with me sometimes. You know how it is, tending bar." Dolan paused. "No, I'd not say he was a friend. I don't believe he ever had a friend—unless it was that kid."

Pete Gaddis shivered. It was the feeling you had, they said, when somebody stepped on your grave.

"There was a kid came to Abilene once, hunting him," Dolan went on. "A few months later Flint showed up. I never did see them together, and down at the stable where the kid worked, the boss said they never talked. Only when Flint disappeared, the kid did, too."

Pete Gaddis took out the brown papers and built a cigarette. He had known Dolan several years and they had talked a lot about guns and cows and liquor and boom towns, but they had never said anything about where or who or how. It was a strange thing that never until now had they touched upon anything they had in common.

"A man like that can't have friends," Gaddis said. "Even a friend can be trusted so far. I doubt if a man in that business would have many friends." Gaddis changed the subject. "This Buckdun—did he ride south?"

Dolan looked carefully at his cigar. I don't know," he said. "I made it a point."

Gaddis downed the last of his whiskey. He drank very little, taking his time with every drink. He took a last drag on the cigarette and dropped it in the sawdust and rubbed it out carefully with his boot toe.

"Bud was in—you know that long, thin galoot who rides for Nugent? He was some liquored up and he was telling us something about a stranger who backed Tom Nugent down."

"A stranger, you say?"

"Big, dark man who backed his talk with a fancy shotgun. Told Nugent he didn't like to have his sleep disturbed, and when Nugent ordered him off the land he told him to go to hell."

Gaddis chuckled. "I'd like to have seen that. Nugent's a fire-eater."

"This time he backed right up."

Pete Gaddis pulled his hatbrim down and walked

out of the Divide Saloon into the evening. A stranger. Of course there were a lot of strangers around.

He walked across the street to the restaurant, thinking about that stranger. Tom Nugent's activities were well known, and, if he had met the stranger, it had been over east, beyond Ceboletta Mesa the night he was chasing down those squatters.

That meant, if the stranger was the man to whom he had talked near the lava beds, that the stranger was working his way west.

But from where he had encountered him, always allowing it was the same man, he must have headed south. Nothing could cross the lava and nobody like him had showed up in Alamitos. And there was nothing to the south until Horse Springs, and the plains where Kaybar cattle grazed.

Suppose more than one gunman had been imported? Suppose this man who was sandy enough to buck Tom Nugent and back him down was a killer imported to kill—whom?

Nancy?

Unlikely. Not many men would kill a woman, and he doubted if a killer could even be hired to do it.

Ed Flynn...

Here he was on surer ground, and the thought worried him. If he only knew where the man had come from. Or if he had a look at him. Bud had seen him.

And if he knew Bud, he would be in town tonight. Bud was a tough hand, but one who liked his bottle.

Flynn was gone, anyway. He had headed for Santa Fe to file those claims.

Pete Gaddis settled down to wait.

IT WAS THE third day before Kettleman managed to get the mare to take sugar from his hand, but once she did she allowed him to pet her, and within the hour he had a bridle on her, and then a saddle.

She humped her back a little at the saddle, but not much, and he petted her and talked to her.

The big red stallion did not approve. He blew and shook his mane and pawed earth. He ran up, then ran away. He was furious, but he was also afraid. Undoubtedly he was puzzled, too, for the mare was unexcited and even seemed pleased at what was happening.

He curried the mare, cleaned the burrs from her tail, and cleaned her hooves. It had been a long time since he had helped shoe a horse but he knew how it was done.

When he got into the saddle the mare did not even buck. She was old, but more important there was a vague memory in her mind of other days when she had been well treated and cared for and there had been grain to eat, and always the sugar. He rode her around the oval, then back to the tunnel.

He was going to ride the mare to Horse Springs, but even as he sat the saddle, he was looking at that big red stallion. He had never seen a more beautiful horse—and the way it moved!

There was a black that looked good, and a big steeldust, almost as big as the red stallion and perhaps a year or two younger.

The stage station at Horse Springs was a low building with an awning supported by posts sunk in the ground. Wind and weather had battered the unpainted structure, fading the few signs and reducing the color to a nondescript gray.

A half dozen other buildings had gone up in the vicinity, a couple of which had been abandoned and now stood empty. The main station was occupied by the saloon, post office, and general store operated by Sulphur Tom Whalen.

Sulphur Tom had his name from the dozens of stories he had to tell of his youth on the Sulphur River of northeast Texas and of such gunfighters as Cullen Baker, Bob Lee, and the participants in the Five County feuds.

He was a tall man, his high, thin shoulders stooped and crossed by suspenders over a red flannel undershirt. He rarely shaved, and his sandy walrus mustache was stained by tobacco. For a man with so many stories of gun battles to tell, Sulphur Tom was remarkable for his own skill in avoiding trouble.

His strict neutrality was backed up by a conveniently located shotgun which he had never used so far as anyone knew. Even when raiding Apaches came around he managed to remain neutral by offering them gifts of sugar and tobacco.

As a normal thing three or four loafers squatted on their heels under the awning or, if the weather permitted, alongside the fence of the nearby corral. There, amid much smoking and spitting, they lied about horses they had broken, steers they had branded, and bears they had killed.

Only two of the four were holding down the position outside the door when the man called Kettleman appeared. He came from the west and he was riding an old mare and she was walking.

When the big man in the flat-heeled boots swung down at Horse Springs, eyes went from him to the ancient brand on the mare. The brand was a fair representation of a six-shooter.

He stepped down from the saddle and, without a glance at the waiting men, went inside. Sulphur Tom had been at the door, but he retreated to his bar and waited. The stranger ignored the bar.

"I'm calling for mail," he said, "mail and a large box."

Sulphur Tom veiled his eyes. "Name?"

"Jim Flint," he said quietly.

Sulphur Tom had his head down, washing a glass, and he completed the job before he looked up. He looked straight at the newcomer. Guiltily, he averted his eyes.

"Been expectin' you," he said. He went behind the barred window that did duty for a post office and took several letters from an open box.

The man who now intended to be known as Jim Flint merely glanced at them and thrust them into an inside pocket of his coat. He looked around, then indicated some saddlebags. "I'll take those, and I can use a couple of burlap bags, if you have them."

"Reckon I do." Sulphur Tom took down the saddlebags from their hook and from under a counter he extracted several burlap bags. His eyes strayed to the mare outside. "Unusual brand," he commented.

Cold eyes measured him. "Is it?"

Mentally, Sulphur Tom backed up. Whatever he was about to say went unsaid. His mouth was dry and something inside him felt queasy. There was something about the big man's expression that he didn't like ... he didn't like it at all.

Sulphur Tom indicated a box on the floor. "There she is," he said, "but you'll pay hell packin' it on a horse."

Stooping, Jim Flint lifted the box easily and swung it to his hipbone. Then he walked outside and, taking the bridle reins, he led the horse across the street to the corral. Around the corner and out of sight of the corral he broke open the box and transferred its contents to the saddlebags and the burlap sacks. Loading them on the horse he walked back across the street and stopped again at the station.

He put an order on the counter and pushed it toward Sulphur Tom. "Fill that," he said, and, turning, he walked to the door.

The two men squatting against the wall were talking idly. "Folks say it's him, all right. Man! I never expected to see nobody like him out here! Why, Buckdun is a known man! He's famous as Wild Bill or Clay Allison, or any of them. There's some say he's killed more men than all of them put together!"

"Shot 'em in the back," the other said contemptuously.

"So he shot from ambush—he killed 'em, didn't he?" He paused. "I wonder who he's to kill out here?"

Flint walked back to the counter where Sulphur Tom was piling the supplies. "I'll eat a can of those peaches here," he said, and opened a can and began to spear them with his knife blade.

When the mail and the box had arrived for Jim

Flint, Sulphur Tom had been excited. He had never known Flint, but Sulphur Tom had had a friend who sometimes kept mail for the gunfighter and received money from him. It had been a good thing, and Sulphur Tom thought he might do the same.

More than the money he wanted the association. Like many another man before him he liked the connection with a big-name man, and liked to have secret information. He was not a talker, but it pleased him to know what others did not.

At first glance he felt a sharp sense of disappointment. This man was too young, and there was a pale shade beneath the sunburn that told of a face long sheltered. Then he remembered how it was that a man might be kept from the sun for years.

Prison.

This man could not be *the* Flint. He was too young. What had Flint's first name been? He could not recall that he ever heard of him as anything but Flint.

How old had he been?

Come to think of it, he did not know. He had never seen Flint, but he had always surmised him to be a man in his thirties or forties, and that had been a long time ago. He stole another look at the man eating the peaches.

It could be. It just could be.

"A handy man," he said aloud, "might make himself some money hereabouts. There's trouble breeding."

As no reply was forthcoming, he added, "Knowed of a man who favored that Six-Shooter brand—but that was long ago."

"Old things are best forgotten." Flint got down from the counter where he had been seated while eating the peaches and went out to the water trough to rinse off his hands. He dried them on his jeans, glancing up the trail as he did so.

Riders were coming. Four of them.

He went back into the store, suddenly irritable at being found here by strangers. The last thing he wanted was to arouse curiosity. The fewer people who knew of his presence the better.

He looked around the store. New York seemed far, far away. The man who had been James T. Kettleman seemed a total stranger. Already he was thinking of himself as Jim Flint.

He looked at himself in a fly-specked mirror, and saw nothing there that looked like death, yet he knew that death was looking back at him. It was unbelievable that a man who had always been so strong could die so simply, yet it was happening.

Despite this thing inside him that was slowly eating away his life, he had always been a man who lived with his muscles as much as with his brain. He had never been ill.

From the day he arrived in New York he had continued his activity, going every day to the gymnasium. He had boxed, wrestled, played handball. And in that second year in New York, before he had begun to win some reputation in the business world, he had fought several times in the prize ring. It had helped to build the capital that finally won success.

He had fought Jack Rooke, an English fighter, meeting him at Bull's Ferry in New Jersey, and whipping him in six minutes with the bare knuckles. He had the Englishman down five times before the end.

A month later he fought ninety-five rounds with Hen Winkle, before the crowd broke down the ropes to save their favorite, Winkle, from a knockout. The fight lasted over two hours.

Two months later, for a thousand-dollar side-bet, he defeated Butt Reilly, knocking him out after one hour of fighting.

He fought four times during the following year, his last bout being at Fox's American Theatre in Philadelphia, where he won from John Dwyer in nineteen minutes.

After that there was no more time for fighting, for his business was developing rapidly. But he had continued to work out in the gymnasiums, to box occasionally with Mike Donovan or Dominick McCafferty, to wrestle a little, and play handball. There had been no hint of this thing that lay within him.

The door swung open and the four riders came in. Flint glanced at them briefly and saw trouble. The first two were swaggering youngsters with uncut hair and dirty range clothes, just out of their teens. One of the two older men was a Mexican, the other a tough, competent-looking man dressed simply, neatly.

"Hey!" one of the younger men yelled at Sulphur Tom. "Give us a drink!"

"Soon's I finish this order," Tom replied shortly.

The young man came down the bar, hunting trouble. "Look, old man," he said, "I reckon you didn't hear me. I said I wanted a drink. And I want it now."

Something seemed to rise inside of Jim Flint. Was it

bitterness that this tough youngster was going to live when he knew he was going to die? Or was it that old love of battle? For nothing else was left to him now.

Or was it that he hoped and wanted to be killed?

"He's waiting on me," Flint said roughly. "You take your turn."

The young man turned like a cat. "Why, you—!"

The sentence was never completed. Jim Flint, far from the marts of capital and bonds, struck viciously.

The young man had started to move in, and the punch caught him flush on his completely unprotected chin.

He hit the floor on his face, as if struck with a mallet.

Jim Flint looked across the fallen man at the three who were with him. "He was hunting trouble. He found it. There's more if you want to buy."

The other youngster started to speak, but the older, neatly dressed man interrupted. "You're quick," he said, "and you hit hard. How are you with a gun?"

Flint looked across the room and said coolly, "As you see, I am wearing one. If you wish to know how good I am with it, you will have to pay to learn."

There had been no move from the man on the floor. The rider who had asked his question had his answer. So he looked down at the fallen man. "Is he dead?"

"I doubt it." Over his shoulder, Flint said to Sulphur Tom, "Get their drinks. I'll buy."

The Mexican walked over and turned the boy over with his boot toe. The youngster blinked, and started to sit up, then sank back with a groan.

"Better take his gun," Sulphur Tom suggested. "He'll be sore as a stepped-on snake."

"Let him keep it," Flint said. "He can do what he likes."

Sulphur Tom took down a bottle and filled glasses for them. "Fill one for him, too," Flint said.

Slowly, the boy on the floor sat up, blinking. He put his hand to his jaw, then stared around him, suddenly remembering.

"You're wearing a gun," Flint said coldly, "and there's a drink on the bar for you. Take whichever one you've a mind to."

Getting awkwardly to his feet, the boy turned his back on Flint and stood there for a moment, swaying uncertainly. Then he stepped over to the bar and took his drink.

When they had finished the four went out and rode away.

Sulphur Tom sacked up the supplies. "You don't take much prodding, do you?"

Jim Flint looked around. "I've got an edge," he said quietly, "because I just don't give a damn."

Taking up the sack, he walked outside and over to his horse. The four riders were nowhere in sight. He loaded the pack and stepped into the saddle. The old mare was carrying a bit of weight, but she was in good shape, and he planned to walk a large part of the distance.

He was not at all sure that the four riders might not be watching the town to see which direction he chose. He rode west, the great open Plains of St. Augustine on his left. Holding close to the mountain, he turned suddenly into Patterson Canyon for a short distance, then took a narrow Indian trial over the mountain to Mangas Canyon.

Several times he stopped to listen, but heard nothing. Before descending into Mangas Canyon he studied the shadowing terrain for some time. Across the canyon and tucked into a draw he saw a clump of trees and he watched it for several minutes. Then he went down the mountain, across the trail and, rounding a boulder found himself in a hollow among the pines that offered a hidden camp where his fire would not show beyond its immediate area.

He had scarcely stopped when the pains seized him and he doubled up, retching violently. He fell to his knees and stayed there, head hanging, for some time, fighting back the groans that came to his lips. When he finally got up he stripped packs and saddle from the mare. Then, putting a hackamore on her, he picketed her on the grass.

He got a small fire going and heated a can of beans. He ate them from the can, and after awhile the pains were less. He thought of New York and his life there. It seemed a far-off thing, another world.

They would be wondering what had become of him, for the two weeks of his planned absence were over. Lottie and her father would be pleased and would rush immediately to the bank. He was amused at the thought of their consternation when they discovered the true state of his affairs.

He heard the horse for several seconds before he became consciously aware of the hoofbeats on the canyon trail. He grasped his rifle and slipped back into the darkness.

Then he heard the approaching horse turn from

the trail and come toward his camp. Suddenly it was there, ears pricked, just beyond the fire.

Its rider was slumped over the saddlehorn, and Flint saw that his wrists were loosely tied to the pommel.

CHAPTER 5

CUTTING THE ROPES, he lifted the man from the saddle and carried him to the fire-light. Then he tied the horse and returned to the man.

He was stocky, powerfully built, at least fifty, wearing a black broadcloth suit, quite dusty now, and dusty cow-country boots that had lately been polished. The inside of his coat and shirt were caked with dried blood from a wound that had bled and then bled again, but he was alive.

He ripped away the bloody shirt. A bullet had gone through the man's side and from the look of it, could have punctured a lung. It was not until he began washing away the blood that he found a second and a third bullet hole.

The second bullet had cut through the man's biceps and penetrated the top of his chest, emerging at the back. The third was lower down. All three wounds were on the left side.

The wounded man muttered, but no words could be distinguished. Going through his pockets Flint found a letter addressed to Ed Flynn at the Kaybar Ranch. The Kaybar. That was the ranch where Gaddis worked.

In each case the bullet had emerged at a point lower than the point of entry. Whoever had done the shooting had been above the rider, which indicated the marksman must have been lying in wait. Which might mean the marksman had been Buckdun.

The wounded man's rifle was unfired, but his pistol had been fired four times.

Flynn had tried. He had shot back at his attacker. From the appearance of the wounds he had been shot as much as a day and a night earlier, and tied his own wrists, hoping his horse would take him back to the Kaybar.

Jim Flint removed some of the sticks from the fire, keeping only the coals to heat water. He bathed the wounds and bandaged them, then made some soup and managed to get the wounded man to take a few mouthfuls.

Twice during the night Flint heard riders pass along the Horse Springs Trail. At daybreak he fed the wounded man a little more soup, and ate some himself.

He was at least thirty miles from the Kaybar headquarters, judging by the map and, encumbered by a wounded man, the ride would take many hours. At any time he might encounter men he did not wish to see, yet he could not abandon the man. Flynn needed a kind of care and medical attention he was not equipped to give, and Flynn's life depended on Flint.

He had gone only a few miles when he saw riders approaching. Far-off there were three riders, and close by, four. And the four were the men he had seen at Horse Springs.

Flint slipped the rawhide thong from the holstered gun and eased the pistol in his waistband. There was no chance of making a run for it and he had no intention of running, anyway. They were coming up on him and it was obvious they meant to stop him. They wanted a fight or they wanted Flynn dead. One of them was returning a pair of field glasses to his saddlebags.

Boldness was the only policy now. He turned his mount and rode straight up to them.

The man he had struck, the long-haired one, was grinning widely. "You again. I been wanting to meet up with you."

Suddenly, as clearly as if he had seen it in print, he knew they meant to kill him, and Flynn, too. A cold fury washed over him suddenly, almost blinding him, and then it passed on and he was left cold, ready, dangerous.

"You'll meet me once too often," he replied shortly. He stepped the mare toward them. "All right, what the hell do you want?"

His violence shocked them. They had been so sure they commanded the situation. He saw the long-haired one sidestep his horse a little, and he saw the older, cooler man place a hand in proximity to his gun. Only the Mexican had made no move. He was looking at Flint with careful, waiting eyes.

"You ain't so tough." The long-haired one wanted to swagger a little. "We're going to kill both you and him."

They were talking up a killing and he did not wait for them to get ready. He shot the long-haired one through the stomach.

His draw was unexpected. They had expected him to talk, perhaps to try to talk them out of it. They were expecting words and he gave them lead. He drew and fired so swiftly it caught them flat-footed.

The man he had shot sat very still, then slid from the saddle and hit the ground with a small thud.

Flint looked at them through the curl of smoke from his gun. "All right. Who's next?"

The Mexican's eyes were steady, but he lifted his hands to shoulder height and backed his horse a step.

The other two sat very still, looking at him. They were not afraid, nor was the Mexican, and of them all, Flint thought, the Mexican had understood most. The fallen man moaned softly, whimpering like a baby.

"I know what you're here for, and take it from me, you're in the wrong business. My advice to you is to get out of the country." He gestured at the fallen man. "You can't help him, but you can try. And after that, bury him and ride out."

The other riders he had seen were coming, so he walked his horse away, leading Flynn's mount. The newcomers were two men and a girl. One of the men was Pete Gaddis, whom he remembered from the moment in the matchlight, the other a young Mexican.

He drew up, waiting for them. He saw Pete Gaddis's eyes go to the brand on his horse, and pause there. When they lifted to meet Flint's, he was shocked by their expression. Gaddis's face showed white under the weather-beaten skin.

Nancy Kerrigan rode quickly to the wounded man. "Ed! Ed! Is it you?"

"He came to my camp. I did what I could but he's in a bad way."

She looked up at Flint and for the first time she realized he was someone she had seen before.

"I know you," she said, "I . . ."

"We have never met," he said brusquely. "You had better see to this man. He will need a doctor."

The young Mexican rider took the lead rope and started off toward the north, wasting no time. Nancy Kerrigan started to speak, then changed her mind and rode away.

Pete Gaddis lingered. "We heard a shot."

"Yes."

Gaddis glanced to the four horses and the men who gathered around the dead man. His eyes returned to the horse and its brand. It was an old brand. And this was an old horse.

"Your voice is familiar. We had a talk once, I believe."

"Yes."

"Only then you didn't have a horse."

"Didn't I?"

Gaddis indicated the men gathered below. "They look like Baldwin riders. Did they shoot Ed?"

"He was shot by someone with a high-powered rifle who was slightly above him, and he was on a horse at the time. He was ambushed."

"How do you figure he was on a horse?"

"Line up the holes in his clothes with the wounds, and you'll see he had to be, and the only way a man can shoot down on a mounted man is to be up higher—in rocks, maybe. Or on a ridge."

Gaddis indicated the group below. "Did they jump you?"

Flint glanced at them. "They were working up to it, but I never could see any sense in talking when it's a shooting matter." He gathered the reins. "This isn't my affair, and I wanted no part of it."

"No matter how it was before," Gaddis said dryly, "you'd better take another look. It's your fight now. They'll make it your fight."

Flint turned his mare. "Adios," he said, and rode away.

Pete Gaddis took out the makings and started to build a smoke. He knew it was impossible, and yet it had to be that way.

And after all this time, too.

CHAPTER 6

H E AWAKENED IN a cold sweat, awakened suddenly and sharply, chilled through and through, and when he fought himself to a sitting position and crawled from the bunk to the fireplace, his teeth were rattling with cold.

Desperately, his hands shaking, he threw together the materials for a fire. The match flickered briefly and then went out.

Almost crying with cold, he struck another, shielded it in his hands until the flame caught. The yellow tongue reached out, lapped curiously at the pine bark, then, catching hold, it crackled with excitement.

The fire brought weird shadows to the cold walls, shadows that made grotesque thumbs at him, but the cold retreated and warmth came as he crouched before the fire, wrapped in blankets. And then the retching started.

He went outside into the white moonlight and clung to the door post and vomited terribly, and there was blood mingled with the vomit. He clung to the door for a long time, too weak to get back inside, and the sweat dried on his body and the white moon looked down upon the jagged black lava that walled his home.

After a while he staggered back to the fire, replenished it, and dozed before it until day came.

At dawn Flint made the beef broth that seemed better for him than anything else. The pain in his stomach grew less but it did not leave and he rested the day through, reading from a book of poetry.

The horses were accustomed to his presence now. Even Big Red failed to blow his warning. Sometimes they would feed up to within a few feet of him, and the mare was always around, begging for sugar. Today he even teased the stallion into taking sugar. The red horse refused it from his hands but, after he left it on a flat rock, came to get it.

He had no regrets for the shooting. He had wanted to avoid trouble, but they had brought it to him, and they had intended to kill Flynn as well as himself.

The warm sun felt good. He read, dozed, then awakened to read again. There was so much he had always wanted to read...

Later he spaded up a small garden patch, and planted several rows of vegetables, beans, carrots, onions, and potatoes. He might not live to enjoy them, but he might become so weak before he died he could not leave the hideout for more food.

Soon he must go to Alamitos.

NANCY KERRIGAN SAT at her desk. Flynn was still unconscious and she had no idea whether he had filed the claims or not. But she had started work on the cabins, and one of her hands who had been a farmer would break the ground for crops.

Gaddis was seated nearby. In reply to a question he

answered, "No, ma'am, I ain't seen him since that day and, whoever he is, I figure he wants to be left alone."

"I have a feeling I have seen him before."

"Yes, ma'am, he has that look about him. He looks familiar to me, too. My advice is to leave him alone."

"Why hasn't he been seen? Where is he?"

"I been puzzling about that. Johnny and me, we tried to trail him." He took out the makings. "Mind if I smoke, ma'am?" He built a cigarette. At the blacksmith shop somebody was working and the afternoon was made more pleasant by the distant ringing of the hammer. "Lost his trail, and he meant that we should. He drops clean out of sight when he takes a notion."

"He talks like an educated man."

"He's educated, all right. He educated them riders of Port Baldwin's, too. I hear talk around town, and they say he got that gun out so fast he caught them flat-footed. And once he got it out he didn't waste no time talking." Gaddis drew on his cigarette. "Interesting thing. He picked up a package and some mail down to Horse Springs that day."

"Have you heard his name?"

The crunch of a boot on gravel was Johnny Otero in the office door. "I can tell you that. Sulphur Tom told me. His name is Jim Flint."

Flint!

Pete Gaddis came half off his chair. So there it was, then. Red Dolan . . . he must get Dolan a chance to see Flint. It was impossible, though. Flint must have had ten or twelve bullets in him.

"Two of Nugent's hands quit him," Johnny volunteered. "Said they weren't drawing fighting pay and to hell with it."

"Tom Nugent's in for trouble, bucking Baldwin. This Baldwin isn't wasting no time."

"And Baldwin started. He pushed five thousand head on to Nugent range today."

Nancy listened, thinking of what she could do if five thousand head were pushed on her range. She was sure that Baldwin had paid the men who squatted on Nugent range, and for the purpose of alienating the squatters and land-seekers coming west. When that got around there would be small sympathy for Tom Nugent.

Yet her thoughts would not remain on the ranch problems or ranch work. She kept remembering the tall man on the old mare. He had seemed so alone. Long after Johnny and Pete returned to the bunkhouse she sat watching the sunset. He had said so few words, and then had ridden away. She detected some strangeness in Pete's reaction to him that puzzled her.

It had been a long time since she had thought about a man, but she told herself that she was merely curious. Yet he was good-looking. Even more—strikingly handsome, and without any softness in him. He looked cold, hard . . . yet was he?

Miles away Jim Flint was watching that same sunset from the hidden pasture. Big Red was feeding close by and seemed glad of the company. He was determined to ride the stallion, but knew his stomach would not stand the pounding of a hard ride, even if he was rider enough to handle such a horse. But there was another and better way. That was with proximity, with gentleness, and casual handling.

His thoughts turned to Nancy Kerrigan. She was

the girl he had seen on the train, but sitting her saddle out there on North Plain, she had seemed even more poised and beautiful.

Yet she was right in the middle of a first-class range war where no girl of her years had any right to be. It was lucky she had Gaddis. He was a fighter. He was also a steady man and no fool. Yet how much of a tactician was he?

Port Baldwin was an old he-coon from the high-up hills when it came to fighting. He had been one of Tom Poole's shoulder-strikers in the old gang-war days of politics—a brutal, confident man who fought to win and would stop at nothing.

That he had brains was obvious by the fact that he had risen from the crowd. There were few shady practices in which Baldwin had not taken a hand. Now he looked and acted the gentleman when it served his purpose, but he had won many a bloody brawl in the streets when he was getting started. At forty, Baldwin was as dangerous and cold-blooded an opponent as a man could find.

On the morning of the third day after the shooting on North Plain, Flint awakened with an itch to get out, to see the newspapers. By now it would be known that he had vanished and questions would be asked.

This time he would go to Alamitos and get the boxes he had there. Besides, he must bring in more supplies. Any day he might become too weak to get out, and he did not want to starve to death.

He saddled the mare and led her through the tunnel. He checked the loads in his rifle and his pistols, for there was every chance that he was riding into trouble.

For a moment he remembered the talk of Buckdun. The man was somewhere around, and it had probably been he who shot at Ed Flynn, and wounded him. There might be others.

Fortunately, he and Baldwin had never met, and Baldwin would not recognize him if they came together on the street.

There were a dozen horses tied to the hitch rail in Alamitos, and two big freight wagons stood near the supply store. Leaving his mare at the rail in front of the stage station which also did duty as a post office, he went inside.

He knew the minute he stepped through the door that the big man in the black suit was Port Baldwin. He was huge, towering inches over six feet, and massively built. His face was wide and there was an old scar on his cheekbone. He looked exactly what he was, a New York tough who had come into money.

Twice in recent years he had taken beatings in stock manipulations, once from Jay Gould, and again from Kettleman. Yet he had forged ahead, using blackmail, threats, and even beatings to frighten his enemies or business rivals.

Walking to the corner, Flint said, "Mail for Jim Flint?" He was aware that Baldwin turned sharply around.

Several letters were awaiting him and he recalled that in the excitement over the shooting on North Plain he had forgotten the mail received on that occasion. The agent said, "There's two big boxes, too."

The door closed behind him and Flint was aware

that the man with Baldwin had gone out. Baldwin stepped up to the counter and turned to face him. "Flint? My name is Port Baldwin, and I want to talk to you."

"Go ahead. You're talking."

"Outside, not here."

Flint turned and looked into Baldwin's cold blue eyes. "Why, sure!" he said. At the door he paused, "You first."

Baldwin hesitated, then stepped through the door. Outside Flint glanced swiftly up and down the street. Three belted men were moving down from the right, two more from the left. A man leaned against a store front across the street.

"You killed one of my men."

"He asked for it."

Baldwin took a diamond-studded cigar case from his pocket and selected one, then handed the case to Flint, who took one. "I want you to work for me," Baldwin said.

"Sorry."

"I'll pay better than anyone else." Baldwin clipped the end from his cigar and put it between his teeth. "I need a man who doesn't waste time. A man who can use a gun."

"No."

Baldwin was patient. "Flint, you simply don't understand. All the rest"—he waved a hand—"they're finished. There's room here for one big outfit, and I'm it."

"Cattle?" Flint asked mildly. "Or is it land?"

Baldwin's pupils shrank, and the muscles around

his eyes tightened. "That's no affair of yours. If you work for me you do as you're told."

"I am not working for you," Flint said quietly. "Nor do I intend to."

"All right." Flint, half-turned to meet the men coming up on him, and too late he saw Baldwin swing. He had not expected Baldwin to take a hand himself, but the big fist caught him behind the ear and Flint fell against the hitch rail, stunned.

Before he could recover his balance or even turn they moved in on him. One man swung viciously at his kidney and a boot toe caught him on the kneecap. He felt the wicked stab of pain and his knee buckled and when Flint threw out an arm to protect himself a man grabbed it and bore down with all his weight. Another grabbed his other arm, and two swung on his unprotected stomach.

Viciously, they pounded him to his knees, and when he fought to his feet, they battered him down again. There was a roaring in his skull and a taste of blood in his mouth. He was falling in the dirt and they were beating, pounding, and kicking him. Yet he could not quit.

Once his fist caught a jaw and knocked a man sprawling. Once he got his toe behind a man's ankle, kicked him on the kneecap with his other heel, and felt the leg bone snap. He grabbed a man behind the neck and butted him in the face. He stabbed a man's nostril with a stiff thumb and felt the flesh tear. But at last they beat him into the dirt and left him there, bloody and broken.

One man remained loafing nearby and, when a

cowhand would have come to Flint's assistance, warned him off.

For more than an hour, Flint lay in the street. Slowly consciousness returned, and with it, pain—a heavy thudding in his skull, and a stabbing in his side. He lay still, aware only of pain, then of the smell of dust, the warmth of the sun on his back and the chill of the ground beneath him, and the taste of blood.

Somehow he knew enough to lie still. He could hear the passing of boots on the boardwalk, the jingle of spurs, a rattling of harness.

Could he move? One hand lay on the ground beneath him, and he tried moving the fingers. They stirred, but stiffly. The back of the hand felt raw, and he seemed to remember it being stamped on. His hand must have been lying on the soft earth near the water trough or the bones would have been broken.

He was in bad shape, but how bad? Had they taken his gun? If he moved now, would he be killed?

Through the fog in his brain, he fought to work out a plan. His head throbbed and his stomach was hot with agony. He worked the fingers in his right hand some more, and opened his eyes to the merest slits.

He was lying just off the walk and because of it he could not see the watcher, although he could hear the creak of the boards when he moved, and the rustle of his clothing. Then Flint remembered the gun in his waistband. Out of sight beneath his coat, they might not have seen it. He worked his hand over to it and grasped the butt.

He did not know whether he could rise or not, but he was going to try. Fury was beginning to build within him. He had always been slow to anger, yet terrible in his rages, for he never ceased to think when angry. He was going to make them pay.

A few faces he remembered, a few hands. Those he wanted. As for Baldwin, there was a better way for him. To such a man defeat is worse than death.

As he was gathering his muscles, a buckboard rounded into the street. He heard the rattle of trace chains, the wheels on the gravel, and then the team drew up.

"What is wrong with that man?" It was Nancy Kerrigan's voice. "Why doesn't somebody do something?"

The watcher replied lazily. "Because he's a man tried to buck Port Baldwin, ma'am. This is the least that happens."

Flint heard the buckboard creak. Then the watcher said, "I wouldn't try that, ma'am. You touch him and I'll have to be rough."

"You are fighting women now?" There was a chill in her voice. "How very brave you must be!"

"We ain't playin' favorites." The man's voice was uneasy. "When he comes out of it, we give it to him again. We keep on doin' that until train time, and then we put the rest of him on the train—if anything is left to put on."

"If you put a hand on me," Nancy Kerrigan said sharply, "I will see you hanged before sundown."

Knowing the watcher's eyes would be on Nancy, Flint rolled swiftly to his knees, gun in hand.

The guard turned swiftly, drawing. Flint fired.

He shot to kill, but his hand was unsteady, his gaze

blurred. The bullet struck the man on the hip, ripping his empty holster loose and knocking him sidewise.

Flint lunged to his feet, swayed dizzily, and caught himself on the hitching rail to prevent a fall.

Another Baldwin man sprang into the street and Flint fired. The bullet ripped splinters from the walk at the man's feet, and another struck the door jamb as he dove for shelter.

The guard was getting up and Flint, swaying drunkenly, cut down with a sweeping blow of his gun barrel that flattened him into the dust. Flint's other pistol was in the gunman's belt. He retrieved it, and took the guard's pistol.

Nancy Kerrigan ran to him. "Oh, please! You're hurt! Get into the buckboard!"

"There isn't time," he said.

He blinked slowly against the pain in his skull, and he swung his head like a huge bear.

The street was emptied of people. Yet they were there, all those who had beaten him. He shifted guns and thumbed shells into the Smith & Wesson.

With a queer, weaving, drunken gait he started up the street. Every breath he took brought a twinge of pain in his side. His head felt like a huge drum in which pain sloshed like water as he moved. He was going to die, and he no longer cared. What he wanted now was to find them. And he knew their faces.

He swayed, half-falling, then pushed himself erect and staggered through the swinging doors of a saloon. The Baldwin riders, some of them at least, were there.

Their laughter died, their half-lifted drinks stopped in mid-air, and Flint fired. He opened up in a blinding roar of gunfire, fanning his gun, for the range was close and there were a number of them.

One man grabbed for a gun and was caught by a bullet that knocked him sprawling. Panic-stricken, another man leaped through a window carrying the glass, frame, and all with him. Another bullet smashed a bottle from a man's hand, and another—it was a face he remembered—struck a man in the spine as he dove for the back door.

Flint staggered to the bar, catching a glimpse of a bloody and broken face in the mirror. He picked up a bottle, took a short drink, and started for the door.

Out on the street he peered right and left. He realized his gun must be empty and holstered it for the guard's pistol.

A window glass broke and a rifle barrel came through. Flint flipped the six-shooter up and snapped a shot through that window. A man sprang from a doorway and fired a quick shot that struck an awning post near Flint.

Flint fired, missed and fired again. The man's knee buckled under him and he scrambled for the door, but Flint fired again and the man cried out sharply and fell forward.

From door to door he went, half-blind with pain and his own blood, dribbling from a lacerated scalp. Twice he almost fell. The men he faced seemed panic-stricken at the sight of him, and they shot too fast or simply ducked out and ran.

Somehow he was back in front of the stage station and his own horse was there. So was Nancy Kerrigan. He had to try twice before he could get a foot in the stirrup and pull himself into the saddle. He swung the mare and started up the street. He began to feed shells into the guard's gun, but it slipped from his fingers and fell into the dust.

He slid forward on the mare's neck, the horizon seemed to bob and vanish into wavering mist, and he felt himself falling. Nancy was beside him. He fell half into the buckboard, and she got down quickly and tipped him over into the back. Tying the mare on behind, she started for the ranch, driving at a rapid clip.

When Flint opened his eyes he was lying in bed between white sheets and staring up at a sunlit ceiling. Slowly, because his neck was stiff, he turned his head.

The room was large, square, and neat. The bed was a huge, old-fashioned fourposter, and there was a dresser and a mirror. The floor was almost painfully clean, polished, and there were several rag rugs. He started to move and felt a twinge of pain in his side that left him gasping. His body felt stiff and when he ran his fingers down his side he found he was taped tightly from armpits to hips.

On a chair back hung his gun belt with a Smith & Wesson in its holster. The other gun lay atop his freshly washed and neatly pressed jeans. His coat hung over the back of the chair also, and in the pocket were the letters.

For several minutes he lay still, luxuriating in the clean sheets. After a while he closed his eyes and slept. When he opened them again he lay looking at his coat and wondering whether the letters were worth the pain of getting them.

He heard footsteps. The door opened and Nancy

came in, looking bright and pretty in a cotton dress of blue and white, carrying herself like a young queen.

"You should see yourself," she said cheerfully. "You're a sight."

"If I look like I feel," Flint said, "I can believe it."

"You're luckier than you have any right to be. The doctor doesn't think there are any broken bones, but he is worried about you. He is afraid you may have internal injuries."

Flint shot her a sharp glance. "Did he give me a thorough check?"

"There wasn't time. He intends to do that when he comes back."

Like hell he will, Flint told himself. "I've got to get out of here," he said. "If Baldwin finds I'm here, you'll be in trouble."

She held the door for a Mexican girl, who brought in a tray of food.

One hand was bandaged, and he decided it must have been the hand that was stamped on. The other hand was bruised and somewhat swollen. When he sat up to eat he caught a glimpse of himself in the mirror, but there was little he recognized.

There was a great welt above one eye and his nose was swollen to almost twice its normal size. His lip and cheek were puffed out in a knot as big as his fist, and there was a cut on his chin. There was a bandage on his skull, and his eyes were scarcely more than slits, but he had expected worse.

"We brought your mare in," Nancy said. "She's out in the stable eating corn like she had forgotten how it tasted." She straightened the bedcovers. "And don't worry about us. If Port Baldwin had not moved in on Tom Nugent he would be here now. We're expecting him."

When she had gone, Flint lay back on the bed. His head was throbbing and he felt very tired.

He had come to New Mexico wanting no trouble. He had wanted no trouble at Horse Springs, and wanted none on North Plain, but long ago he had discovered that one has to make a stand. If a man starts to run, there is nothing to do but keep running. And if a man must die, he could at least die proud of his manhood. It was better to live one day as a lion, than a dozen years as a sheep.

Rolling to his elbow, he got the letters from his pocket. One was from the Baltimore attorney, forwarding papers that indicated his plans in some respects were complete, and some investments had been concluded. The other letter was the final report from the detectives.

Port Baldwin had been the man who arranged for Lottie and her father to secure the services of the gambler who tried to kill him.

And her father had been associated in some of Baldwin's financial schemes.

With difficulty he brought his mind to consideration of the problem. Long ago he had heard of an old Chinese saying to the effect that any man who could concentrate for as much as three minutes on any given problem could rule the world. The thought had remained in his mind, and he had cultivated the ability to apply all his intelligence to any given situation. To close out everything from his mind but the one idea to be considered had taken long practice, but much of his success had been due to that ability to concentrate, to formulate the problem, to bring to it all the information and knowledge he had, and to reach a decision. Only now he was too tired, his head throbbed too much, and he wanted only to rest.

However, and he realized it with surprise, for the first time he was thinking of doing something for someone else.

True, Baldwin had ordered him beaten, but in a measure he had paid him for that. What he wanted to do had no concern with his own feelings. He wanted to help Nancy Kerrigan.

He closed his eyes against the ache in his head, but her image remained with him. How different it might have been had he met such a girl instead of Lottie! But would it? For he was dying now, bit by bit, day by day.

Yet time remained, and he had always loved a good fight. He would help Nancy, he would whip Baldwin, and he would go out with that, at least, completed.

For a man who had fought all his life, it would be best to go out fighting. Too often men were concerned merely with living, even if they must crawl to survive. He would fight Port Baldwin, he would beat him. Nancy would have her ranch, she would...

At some point he went to sleep.

CHAPTER 7

WHEN HE AWOKE it was dark. He could hear the stirrings and the sound of dishes that meant suppertime. Flint sat up and put his feet to the floor.

When Nancy came in he was strapping on his gun belt.

"You're being very foolish," she said severely. "You need rest."

"I'll get all the rest I need soon enough." He paused, looking at her in the half-light. "Right now I'm hungry. Anyway," he added brusquely, "I'm not a man who could ever lie abed when there are things to be done."

He tucked the other pistol into his waistband and donned his coat, following Nancy into the main room. She had lovely shoulders, and when she turned to look at him, it was with a quick, direct gaze.

The ranch house was spacious and comfortable. There were books on some shelves across the room, and he went to look at them. Charles Dickens, Anthony Trollope, Sir Walter Scott, Washington Irving, Shakespeare, Hume's *History of England*.

He was not surprised by the quality of the authors, for he had read the journals of the trappers who came west, and he had known many western men, and knew of the books they read. They could carry few so they carried the best.

Nancy returned to his side. "You are interested in books?" she asked.

"As you've noticed, Miss Kerrigan, I am a lonely man, and such men are inclined to read. Luckily, one of my teachers got me started on Plutarch and Montaigne."

"You're a puzzling man. You give the impression of being educated, and yet—"

"My reactions yesterday disturbed you, is that it? Why do people so readily assume that a man of education cannot also be a man of violence—when violence is called for?

"Christopher Marlowe was put under bond to keep him from beating up the constable on his way home, and Socrates was a soldier as well as a good wrestler. Remember how he threw Alcibiades, who was interrupting his conversations? Threw him and held him down, and Alcibiades was noted for his strength.

"And Ben Jonson. He once met in single combat in the open field between the assembled armies the best fighter in the French forces, and defeated him.

"Believe me, the list is a long one, and many men of education have on occasion been men of violence. An educated man demands his right to information, for example. Take it from him or censor it and he is apt to become violent."

"Are you a western man, Mr. Flint?"

"I suppose. All western men are from somewhere else, when it comes to that. At the stage station in Alamitos I heard German, Swedish, and Irish accents in just a few minutes, but I suppose being a western man is a matter of psychology. The mere fact that a man chooses to come west indicates a difference of temperament or attitude, and then there's bound to be changes due to the landscape and the conditions. I suppose the basic difference is that men want to survive, to mate, and to have security ... and out here the other considerations are outweighed by the necessity to survive."

"Mr. Flint—?"

"Call me Jim. I am used to it."

"All right—Jim. When you found Ed, was he able to talk? He was on a business trip for the ranch, and we don't know whether he was shot when he was going out or coming back."

"He was worried. He muttered something about Santa Fe, and about someone called Gladys, that was all. No, he was never conscious while he was with me."

She led the way to the long table, and he seated her. "Thank you," she said. "That is a courtesy I do not often encounter."

The hands came in slowly and sat down, stealing glances at Flint.

"Would you like to tell me about it?" he asked. "I know you are in trouble. Maybe I can help."

"Porter Baldwin is going to need a lot of land for forty thousand head of cattle," Nancy said. "It's as simple as that."

He needed to ask no more questions. Few pioneer ranchmen had ever filed on their land. Indeed, when many of them settled in the West there was no legal way to file and nobody to dispute their claims but wild Indians. Later, the courts and the congressmen of settled states were inclined to dismiss all the ranchers might have done and open their grazing land to settlement. Such action was not, naturally, appreciated by the cattlemen.

In some cases ranchers had purchased land from Indians, but the government rarely accepted such purchases as legal. Flint was completely aware of all these factors, and knew what the usual steps were.

"Have you had your hands file claims for you?"

She looked up quickly, and he was aware of the sudden attention from down the table.

"Isn't that illegal?" Nancy asked quietly. "But to reply to your question: yes. We have no choice, and if any of the men wish to keep their claims, they may. If not, we will buy their rights from them. It is either that or lose the ranch my father and uncle worked so hard to build."

"There may be other alternatives," Flint replied. "Are you running cattle on railroad land?"

"No, we are not. Tom Nugent does, and some of the others. Of course, Port Baldwin is. But we never have used any of that graze that we know of, as we hold our cattle farther south."

Long after dinner they sat on the wide veranda and listened to Johnny Otero singing near the bunkhouse.

Flint led Nancy to talking of the ranch, and learned the whole story of her efforts to improve it. He was surprised by her appreciation of the grazing problem, and what she had done about it. One of her hands had been a German who remained at the ranch an entire summer making repairs in the house, building cabinets and furniture. He had told her about grazing methods in Germany and Switzerland, and from him she learned the use of spreader dams, dams built to spread the runoff from hillsides instead of letting it trickle away. Wells had been dug, seeps cleaned out, herds trimmed to avoid overgrazing.

"My father was a great believer in children being given responsibility, Jim. He gave me things to do as early as I can remember. And he used to talk to me about the ranch, and explain everything he did, and why he did it.

"You know how children are. They are always curious and they want to know something about everything. I don't remember a single question of mine that he left unanswered. Sometimes when I would ask him something he thought was intelligent he would give me a gift or take me somewhere that I wanted to go.

"He never gave me anything really big that I didn't earn. Sometimes I had to do very little to earn whatever he gave, but it was usually something. Why, before I knew the ABCs I could name every cattle brand in this part of the state, and I could recognize all the plants that poison stock such as loco weed and larkspur."

Long after he lay in bed he thought of her and the long talk on the darkening porch. He could not remember ever talking so long to any one person, not even Flint.

He was very stiff, and no matter how he turned there was a sore spot. For three days he loafed about the ranch, and during all that time he was aware that Pete Gaddis, Johnny Otero, or a hulking brute of a man with a good-natured face, Julius Bent, was always around.

He learned that Baldwin had tried to get a warrant

for his arrest but the local judge refused. "I saw what happened," the judge rasped, "and as far as I am concerned it was justified. It was self-defense."

"He wasn't defending himself," Baldwin replied angrily, "he was attacking!"

"Attack can be the best defense," Judge Hatfield replied grimly. "You had attacked him without provocation, and he had every reason to believe you would attack him again. I am only sorry he stopped shooting when he did."

Baldwin had stalked angrily from the office, and Hatfield had chuckled and returned to his work.

Baldwin was worried, and he did not know why. Shrewd as he was, he often trusted to purely animal instincts, attacking whenever weakness was evident, biding his time when faced with strength, and trusting to a sharp instinct for danger to save him from going too far.

He felt that warning of danger now and it worried him all the more because he was not sure where the danger lay. As he carefully sifted the events of the day through his mind there was one comment that remained. Flint had asked him whether it was cattle he was interested in—or land.

Was that a guess? Or did Flint know something?

The latter was unlikely, yet it did not pay to overlook possibilities. The swiftness of Flint's action both at Horse Springs and on North Plain had shocked Baldwin's men. They were wary of Flint now, and there was an old story being revived—something about another Flint who had been a notorious killer.

Baldwin decided there was something here he did not understand. He was aware that some of his riders believed Flint was insane, especially after he shot up Alamitos.

Baldwin chewed his black cigar thoughtfully, sitting on the edge of his hotel bed in his shirt sleeves. Thus far things had gone according to plan. Flynn was not dead, but his death was not essential, merely that he be out of action. Kaybar was no longer a serious obstacle, and he had taken steps to eliminate Tom Nugent.

Nugent's swift action against the nesters had alienated the feelings of a lot of people at Alamitos. It would stand against him in Socorro or Santa Fe, if it ever came to that. Nugent would have few friends, anyway, for he was a hot-tempered, arrogant man who made enemies. Several of his hands had quit already.

Port Baldwin had come up the hard way. It had been his experience that victory paid off, and losers got exactly nowhere. The government was inclined to a hands-off policy, and a man could get away with as much as he was big enough to handle. Port Baldwin was, he reflected, pretty big.

He had made his money through speculation, intimidation, and conniving, getting in quick and getting out with a profit. The future of the country did not interest him. He thought only of himself and what he could get out of it now.

He had speculated in railroads, town-site developments, in mines and shipping, but the railroad land situation, and the state in which government land stood appealed to his instinct for a fast deal.

Word from Washington was that a change was due in the land laws, and Baldwin foresaw enormous profits for those in possession. But he decided there was a profit to be made without awaiting the legislative action.

He knew it was almost impossible for the railroad to dispose of their land. They had been given the odd-numbered sections along both sides of the railroad right of way, but the cattlemen, accustomed to free range, grazed government and railroad land with equal disregard for ownership, and under the existing laws it was impossible to prevent such trespass.

Where railroad land had been sold the contracts usually stipulated that if the purchaser failed to make payments on schedule all profits from the land in question would revert to the railroad, after default in payment. If payments continued to be defaulted for three months, the land purchase price became due and the company was free to foreclose.

Thousands of land-hungry men were coming west, most of them with a little money to invest, and few of them knowing anything about the land itself. Little of the land in which Baldwin planned to deal could be farmed. It was grazing land, thin-soiled and of value for little else, and to make money from grazing land, thousands of acres were necessary.

Once he had driven the Kaybar and Nugent from their holdings, Baldwin meant to sell the land to dry farmers, using the same contract the railroad used. He had also secured from the railroad tentative approval of a plan to sell their land, and it was this fact he planned to use in advertising land for sale. Most of the buyers would be, he knew, innocent of the procedures of land purchase, and most of them would believe he was selling only railroad land. Others would believe he was selling off the big ranches to which he had obtained title. Few would go to the extent of a title search, and for those few he had methods of persuasion. If they talked too much they would find themselves on a train going east, in an empty boxcar, badly beaten up.

Few would be able to keep up payments on the land they bought, and the land would revert to him. Whenever possible he meant to assure himself of a reasonable title, but Baldwin knew few of the buyers could afford extensive litigation.

Once he had sold the land, he would sell off his cattle and go east, retaining title only to that land on which payment had been defaulted. Quite coolly he planned to sell land to which he had no title at all, knowing that if the matter went to the courts, he would no longer be within their jurisdiction.

It was a swindle, and he regarded it as nothing else, but a swindle it might take years to unravel, and there were always ways of getting such cases delayed or thrown out of court.

Baldwin knew that few of the ranchers in the area had title to the land they grazed, and he had thought of ways to make that fact work for him. Rolling his black cigar in his jaws, Baldwin contemplated the future with satisfaction. He had lost a good bit of money, but this deal would give him more capital, and it would also give him a good deal of collateral.

Flynn was out of it. Nugent soon would be. That Kerrigan girl would cause him no trouble. Pete Gaddis he had estimated and dismissed. Undoubtedly a tough man in a fight, he was no businessman and no leader.

Flint had no real stake in the fight, and his friendship with the Kerrigan girl must be scotched at once. Buckdun could take care of that.

Baldwin was pleased. He allowed himself ninety days to be in complete possession of three million acres.

He picked up his newspaper that had been delivered to his room and took it down to the restaurant. Harriman was in the midst of a fight with the Morgan-Vanderbilt interests, and Kettleman was expected to intervene. Baldwin stared at the name irritably. He had lost money on the Union Pacific stock deal, for he had attempted to follow Kettleman's lead and had been caught short.

Kettleman had been a major stockholder and a director. He gained control of the Kansas Pacific and declared his intention of building another transcontinental railroad to rival the Union Pacific. Frantic at the thought of competition, the Union Pacific moved to buy Kansas Pacific stock. That stock was way below par, and when Kettleman sold he forced the Union Pacific to buy at par, and cleared ten million on the deal.

Port Baldwin learned from Kettleman's father-in-law that Kettleman was buying Kansas Pacific stock. Rushing in, he bought Kansas Pacific himself, but the deal with Union Pacific was made secretly, and Kettleman had sold out before Baldwin knew it. The stock took a nose dive, and Baldwin was all but cleaned out.

Ten million! Baldwin rustled his paper angrily. Every time he thought of it, he was enraged. Lottie would have it all, someday, if she just outlived Kettleman.

How could Kettleman have killed that gambler? The man was notorious on the Mississippi riverboats, and had been hired several times for killings, each of which had gone off successfully. Baldwin had been careful not to be close by, yet from all accounts, the gambler had drawn his pistol and was about to shoot when Kettleman produced a gun as if by magic and killed him.

Baldwin had worried ever since the failure of the attempt. Kettleman had the reputation of a man who did not forget an injury, and it was whispered that the gambler had talked before he died. How much had he talked? That was the question.

Baldwin had seen a chance at a tidy profit. If Kettleman was killed there would be an immediate reaction on the market. Baldwin prepared for it—but lost again.

There was nothing to do now but wait and let Buckdun handle his part of it, and the cattle would do the rest.

Baldwin had never seen Kettleman. For that matter he had never seen Jay Gould or Commodore Vanderbilt, either. He had seen Harriman, a shrewd young man who would go far, and he knew Jim Fisk.

There was time. He was only forty years old and tremendously strong. In the twenty years since he had been a shoulder-striker for Tom Poole he had come a long way. The rest of them: Where were they? Dead or booze hounds, running games, or tending bar.

Jim Flint came into the room and sat down opposite Baldwin. His face was badly discolored and

Baldwin heard murmurs. Not a soul among the twenty or so in the dining room did not know about that beating and how it had come about.

He felt his face growing red and it angered him. What did that fool Flint mean, coming into a hotel dining room? Porter Baldwin felt a slow anger growing within him. Buckdun was the only answer to this man.

Flint looked over at him and smiled a taunting smile. "Hello, Port," he said. "Some day you must try hitting me when my back is not turned."

"I don't brawl."

"I think you're yellow, Port. You hire your fighting done. But you know something, Port? I think you should go back to New York. If you don't go now, you may never make it."

Port Baldwin's appetite was gone, and there seemed to be a chill in the room. It was strange he had not noticed it before.

CHAPTER 8

FLINT DID NOT finish his meal. Brief as was the exchange with Port Baldwin, it left him restless and irritable. He was aware that his whole manner had reverted to what it might have been had he remained in the West.

Outside the night was cool and the stars were out. He glanced to right and left along the street, feeling the old wariness returning.

During the years he had traveled with the first Flint, he had never been without this wariness, although he was never allowed in the vicinity of a killing, nor told exactly what his benefactor was doing. Always, he was left in some lonely spot to care for the horses. It was a good thing to have fresh horses where a man knew they would be.

He felt better after he had eaten. The pains did not bother him so much. Perhaps this was the onset of that feeling of well-being he had been told to expect when the end was drawing near.

He did not feel like a dying man. His mind accepted the verdict, but the blood in his veins flowed as always, and the night wind tasted as good. It was only when the pains came, and the retching, only when he found the blood on his lips that he could believe it with his body as well.

He crossed the walk and stepped into the saddle,

turning downstreet. As he did so a man moved from the shadows not far away and started up the back stairs of the hotel. Flint recognized the tall, lean man from the train and, from talk he had overheard, he figured this would be Buckdun.

On impulse Flint turned his mare sharply and walked her to the foot of the stairs.

"Buckdun!"

The man turned warily. Dimly visible in the faint light from the hotel windows, he peered at Flint from under his hatbrim. Flint knew that his own face was equally invisible, although he sat plainly in the light from the front window of the hotel.

"Buckdun, leave the Kaybar alone. I am telling you now. I will not tell you again."

Buckdun was a man who killed for money, and carefully, with no desire to risk himself. "I don't know as I've heard of the Kaybar," Buckdun replied. "Who might you be?"

"I am Flint."

That name would mean more to Buckdun than the others, for he would know the legend and much of the fact around that name.

"I'd say you were a mite young. Seems to me Flint would be—well, maybe sixty years old now."

"Maybe." Flint turned his mare. "I think we understand each other, Buckdun. This is no challenge, just a piece of advice. I doubt if either of us really wants to fight the other."

He walked the mare down the street and out of town.

Buckdun stood on the shadowed stairs and watched him go. How old had Flint been? The trail crew of the Three-X were supposed to have killed him in the fight at The Crossing, years ago. But no body ever was found. When the lights went on Flint was gone as well as the kid.

This might not be the original Flint, but if a man prepared for the worst he saved himself a lot of trouble.

When Buckdun shot Ed Flynn, he had him dead to rights till Flynn's horse started acting up. It was the first time Buckdun had failed to make a kill. He was not a superstitious man, but there might be a sign in that failure. He had better leave Kaybar alone.

Buckdun went up the stairs to one of the hotel rooms. For an instant he stood inside the door, listening. He was sitting on the bed in the dark when Baldwin came in.

"You sent for me?" Buckdun said.

Baldwin took out a cigar, then offered one to Buckdun, who accepted it. "We have to move faster. I want Tom Nugent."

"All right."

"And I want a Kaybar rider. Choose your own. I want to scare that girl out of there."

"No."

Baldwin looked at him past the glow of a match.

"I've been warned off Kaybar by a man who seems to be interested there."

"Flint? What does it matter? He isn't important."

"Now, that's a question. Mr. Baldwin, there was a man in my business named Flint. That was some years back. That man was a marvel, Mr. Baldwin. Every job was clean and smooth."

"He's dead?"

Briefly, Buckdun outlined the events at The Crossing. "This might be the same man. If he is, and if he starts gunning, he could be a trouble."

"Are you afraid?" Baldwin's tone was sarcastic.

"I am a businessman, Mr. Baldwin, in a business where I cannot do a good job if I have to worry about my back. Whether there is any connection with the old Flint or not, this one is unpredictable, as you have reason to know."

"All right, leave him to me."

"Sure." Buckdun got to his feet. "Mr. Baldwin, I'd lay off the Kaybar if I were you. He might start hunting, and you'd be a sitting duck."

Baldwin started to make an angry reply, but Buckdun interrupted. "You have been standing in front of a lighted window for several minutes. If I had been hunting you, you'd be dead. I take a professional interest, and you ain't used to a rifle country, Mr. Baldwin."

"You take care of Nugent," Baldwin replied sharply. "I will take care of myself."

"All right. But you better pay me for that Flynn job, and my advance on Nugent."

"You don't trust me?"

"This ain't a trusting business, Mr. Baldwin. You don't trust nobody. Especially if they stand in front of windows. I won't get far, Mr. Baldwin, with a claim against your estate."

Buckdun stepped out of the door when his money was paid, closing it so softly there was no sound. Baldwin listened for footsteps, but heard nothing. Taking off his coat and loosening his stiff collar, Baldwin propped a couple of pillows behind him and sat on the bed to think. Flint worried him. Buckdun's odd manner worried him still more, but stirred his impatience, also.

————

FLINT TURNED THE mare out to pasture. The big red horse was feeding close by. Flint held out sugar to him but the red horse would not take it from his fingers, although he accepted it from the flat rock within a yard of Flint.

The second piece the stallion took from his fingers, after stretching his nose toward the sugar several times. Later that afternoon Flint managed to get a hand on the stallion's shoulder, talking to him gently. Still later he rubbed his back and scratched under his mane. Proximity and sugar were slowly winning him over.

That night Flint slept a sound sleep for the first time in months, and awakened thinking of Nancy Kerrigan and their long talks during his stay at the ranch.

He shaved, dressed in fresh clothing, and considered the situation. The thing to do was break Port Baldwin from the New York end. He thought for a minute, weighing possible allies in New York, the voting power of his stock, and other factors.

He saddled the mare, taking time out to pet the stallion, and even to pull himself half on to the red horse's back. The stallion sidestepped a little, but seemed more concerned with getting more sugar than with objecting to the handling. He was quite sure he could ride the red stallion when he wanted to.

Leading the mare, Flint went down the outer passage through the lava, and was within a few yards of the trail when he heard voices. There were seven riders. They were Baldwin men.

Nothing lay in the direction they were taking but the Kaybar, unless they were going to Horse Springs, which was unlikely. Waiting a few minutes, he led the mare out, brushed away the tracks, and stepped into the leather.

The sky was tufted with bits of white cloud, the air was clear, and the sun was warm.

In Alamitos, on that morning, Porter Baldwin was opening a land office, advertising for sale cattle ranches, dry farms, and town-site lots.

In New York, Lottie Kettleman had found out that her husband had disappeared.

Near the lava beds Flint was trailing the seven Baldwin riders. They held to a tight bunch, riding slowly to stir no dust cloud. When they disappeared into the trees beyond North Plain, he took a direction diagonally away from them, but once under cover of the trees he turned north and rode swiftly to make up for time lost.

Their destination was now obvious. They were headed for the Kaybar headquarters. Flint could see the highest peak of the Zuni Mountains dead ahead, and knew that peak lay northwest from the Kaybar.

He thought of attempting to reach the ranch ahead of them, but doubted if the old mare would stand the run.

He rode with extreme care, holding his rifle across the saddle and ready for action. It was a custom-made rifle, built by a man who made weapons for the Grand Duke Alexis and others, and possessed extraordinary range and accuracy.

The Baldwin riders were holding close to the lava beds so he rode wide, using every bit of cover, and gained some ground. He was on the north slope of the Zuni Mountains when he came within sight of Kaybar, and glimpsed a dust cloud far away to the north indicating a second group of riders.

He stepped up his pace, cutting down the hillside and gaining a little ground by virtue of terrain. The riders along the lava beds started to trot their horses, and as if by prearrangement, those at the foot of the Zunis did also.

"All right, girl," he said to the mare, "let's see if you can run."

He walked her out of the trees and started down the slope. He was at the apex of a triangle with riders coming up both sides toward him.

The mare started to trot. So far he had not been seen. Sensing his urgency, she began to go faster and faster. Now they were within sight of the ranch and on level ground. From behind he heard a shout, then a shot. The range was too great and he was not worried, but the mare stretched out and began to run.

At the ranch somebody ran into the yard and he saw sunlight on a rifle barrel. He talked to the mare and, glancing back, saw a rifle leveled. There was a dip in the ground off to the left. He swung over and dropped into it, hearing the bullet go by.

When he came out of the hollow he let the mare have her head and she started running all out, giving it everything she had. Old as she was, she was a fine horse and she loved to run.

Then the others broke from the brush and trees and, stretched out in a long line, swept down on the ranch, guns popping. Somebody fired from the ranch and then he was racing into the yard.

He swung an arm to indicate the attack was coming from all directions and then rode the mare to the stable and, dropping to the ground, ran back.

Johnny Otero was down behind a plank water trough, rifle ready, and Pete Gaddis came running from the bunkhouse carrying an extra cartridge belt.

Otero fired first and a gray horse running full tilt took a header, throwing its rider head over heels to the ground. The rider started to get up, and Otero fired again.

Riders rushed into the ranch yard and one man lifted a gun toward Otero. Flint fired his big game rifle and the man was lifted from the saddle and smashed to the ground. It was close range now. Dropping the rifle, he sprang into the open and emptied his six-shooter into the racing riders. Then he switched guns with a border shift, throwing the empty gun to his left hand, the loaded gun to his right, opening fire so swiftly there was almost no break in the sound.

Two saddles were emptied and a man riding away seemed to turn in the saddle and fall, his foot hanging in the stirrup.

The attack ended abruptly. Flames crackled up from a huge stack of hay. Otero had a bad burn across the top of his shoulder, but the defenders suffered no other injuries. Flint loaded his pistols and recovered his rifle.

At the stable he stripped the saddle from the mare and, taking a handful of hay, gave her a swift rubdown, then threw an old blanket over her. He put grain in the feed box and hay in the manger. He was coming out of the stall when pain seized him, knotting his stomach with agony. He doubled over, and caught the edge of the stall for support, then slid to his knees.

Johnny Otero stepped into the door. "Hey, did you get hit?"

Flint shook his head. Otero waited, uncertain, then backed out and went to the house. Slowly the attack passed. Flint pulled himself erect. He spat. There was blood on the hay.

He walked out of the barn, feeling weak and sick. He squinted his eyes against the sun and stood in the stable door for a minute, trying to fight his way back to composure.

Otero came from the bunkhouse carrying an extra rifle, a second pistol tucked into his waistband. He glanced curiously at Flint. "You all right?" he asked.

"All right," Flint said briefly.

"There's more guns in the house," Otero said.

There was a burst of firing from the west and two riders came at the ranch on a dead run.

"Hold your fire!" Otero yelled. "That's Julius!"

Julius Bent dropped from the saddle in time to catch the other rider as he fell. The wounded man had been shot twice, through the leg, and through the chest.

Flint walked around the ranch yard, studying the situation. The place was in good shape as long as daylight held, but with the small number of men they had to defend it, night attack was sure to end in disaster. The attackers could close in under cover of darkness and fire the buildings, then shoot down the defenders as they emerged.

No help could be expected from the outside. If Baldwin had thought to guard the telegraph station it was doubtful if the territorial government would know of what was going on until the fight was over, and then Baldwin could say it was a fight between the big ranches and squatters.

The telegraph station...

Jim Flint paused in his pacing. The place to beat Baldwin was New York. The telegraph made it almost next door.

He went to the house. "We've got to get out of here, as soon as it's dark," he told Nancy.

Gaddis nodded agreement. "He's right. They'll burn this place tonight whether we are in it or not."

Burn the ranch? Nancy looked slowly around her, scarcely able to imagine life without this house. She had grown up here. There were marks of her uncle and father all around. Yet she knew that what Flint and Gaddis said was true.

"We will need all the grub we can get together," she said, "and packhorses. I doubt if they will expect us to run."

"Where'll we go?" Gaddis asked mildly.

"There is only one place," Nancy said. "We will go to the Hole-in-the-Wall." She turned to explain to Flint. "It's a lava-walled pasture—twelve thousand acres of it. I doubt if any of Baldwin's men know it exists."

Flint watched Nancy. He knew what this meant to her. This home was her life, her memories, all she had.

"We will have to take Flynn," she said, "and Lee Thomas."

Thomas, the wounded rider, grinned at Flint. "Hell, you get me on a horse, that's all I ask. I rode twenty miles through a blizzard one time with a broke leg."

When they were alone, Nancy turned to him. "Jim. I'm glad you're here."

"Yes," he said. "I wouldn't want to be anywhere else."

At her quick glance, he added, "At a time like this."

He walked outside. The sun was a ball of fire over the Continental Divide.

"You'll make a fool of yourself," he said aloud, "if you aren't careful."

CHAPTER 9

LOTTIE KETTLEMAN STOOD rigidly before the bank window. "I do not understand you," she protested. She was very pale. Inwardly she seethed with anger. "I . . ."

"I am sorry, Mrs. Kettleman." The cashier's manner was polite, but shaded with coolness. "Mr. Kettleman closed his account several weeks ago."

He hesitated, ashamed of his feeling of satisfaction. This woman had always been arrogant, imperious, difficult. "It was just before Mr. Kettleman left for Virginia."

She turned quickly and left. She was filled with vindictive anger, but she was also frightened. Only this morning, using the key her father secretly had had made for her, she had opened the safe at home. It was empty.

She got into a hansom cab and raged at its slowness until she reached Burroughs's office. She was shown in at once.

"He left an allowance for you." Burroughs carefully kept all expression from his face. "You are to be paid one hundred dollars a month for twelve months."

"What?" She fought to keep her poise. "But where *is* he? What does this mean?"

Burroughs shuffled papers on his desk. "Mr.

Kettleman never confided in anyone, but it has been apparent for several weeks that he was arranging his affairs for an extended absence. It may be"— Burroughs kept his expression bland—"that he suspects a plot against his life. It seems there was an incident at Saratoga where a man tried to kill him."

"That's absurd! It was just a gambling argument."

"As I have said, he did not confide in me, but I happen to know he retained the Pinkertons for an investigation. That was unusual, to say the least for, as you were no doubt aware, Mr. Kettleman maintained his own private organization."

She had known nothing of the kind. Her throat tightened, and she thought back swiftly. There were no letters. Meetings, yes. And with Baldwin—but how could he learn of that?

"How does he expect me to live on one hundred dollars a month?" she protested.

"Many families do," Burroughs replied, remembering he had been married on considerably less. "You have a beautiful home, and there is always"— he cleared his throat—"your father."

Lottie Kettleman shot him an angry glance. Was he being sarcastic?

"You have no idea where he is?"

"No, I have not."

Lottie Kettleman arrived home frightened and furious. For the first time she began to think seriously about the man she had married.

Kettleman, her father assured her, was a lonely man without family ties. He had never known a home, and would be easy pickings for a clever girl. Once married to him she would have access to his private papers, the confidences that were natural between husband and wife, and she could supply tips to her father and his associates by which they could make millions.

It was not the first time she had assisted her father in his schemes, and this seemed more practical than most of them. Moreover, Kettleman was handsome, distinguished-looking, as well as both feared and respected in financial circles.

It was only after they were married that she discovered he never discussed business at home and kept his affairs in his head. The few notations she could find were in some private code known only to him.

Her father had taken an impression of the key to the safe and they had one made for it. Together they opened the safe and found in it only a few stacks of carefully specified bills. It was the way of James T. Kettleman to keep his cash so. Neatly piled with the number of bills and amount atop it. The only other objects in the safe were a worn gun belt and a Navy Colt.

When she opened the safe that morning to find the money gone, the gun and gun belt were gone, too. She assumed the gun was one he would want when he went hunting, and gave it no thought.

Kettleman had been attentive and thoughtful, but she had never loved him and he soon discovered it. He also learned that he had mistaken his own desire for a home and family for love of her. They lived in the same house but there had been only politeness between them. After the shooting at Saratoga he had returned to the house only occasionally, and rarely stayed long.

Even before her visit to the bank she had detected a

coolness about town, and she began to understand what she was facing.

She loved her father but for the first time she realized that his grandiose schemes would never come to anything. Lately he had begun to whine and blame his failures on others.

For the first time she began to appreciate Kettleman—or rather, the life he had given her. There had been no worry about bills, she had been treated everywhere with respect, and she had not been curious enough to try to know him.

He was a means to money. Otherwise she was indifferent. Now she realized he was a mystery, and not only to her. Nobody knew anything about him or his background.

Nor was there any clue as to what had become of him. He seemed to have dropped off the world as if he had never been. With her father she went to the Virginia farm.

The house was closed and locked. Forcing a way in they could find no evidence that he had been there in some time. The few neighbors were remote and only one of them had known him slightly, but he had not seen him in more than a year.

Back in New York she paced the floor angrily. Her father, a large, heavyset man, puffed a cigar. For the first time Lottie was seeing him as a ponderous, shoddy man with a little cunning and an easy flow of talk.

"He called in the Pinkertons, did he? Well, why don't we do the same? Mind you, girl, when we find him we will find money. He has something of consequence in mind. There's a man named Epperman, a

German. He's done some investigative work for Port Baldwin, time to time."

———

EPPERMAN SAT BACK in a squeaky swivel chair and considered the project. Then he made inquiries. No. There was no picture. Kettleman had never wanted a picture made.

To Epperman this smelled of money. If Kettleman had disappeared it was something another client of his should know. A canny man might make much of such knowledge.

Epperman was a stocky man with a florid face and rather protruding eyes of pale blue. He observed Lottie Kettleman's lush figure with appreciation. A likely filly and, from rumor, no better than she had to be.

A week around financial circles brought Epperman no news. Everybody knew Kettleman, but no one offered a clue. There was no criminal record. He started to work back toward the beginning. Among other things, he discovered that Baldwin, often a client of his, had lost money in several deals in which Kettleman was involved. And also that Peres Chivington, Lottie's father, had supplied information to Baldwin, a time or two.

He had been working on the case for more than a week when he stumbled on a surprise. Kettleman had belonged to a shooting club and was a remarkably good shot. He was also a handy man with his fists, someone said. Another voice said, "He was a prize-fighter, I think."

In one of the old hangouts of the Morrissey crowd

Epperman found a whiskey-soaked old-timer who said, "Jim Kettleman? If you want to know if he could fight, ask Dwyer, him that was bare-knuckle champion."

Inquiry developed that Kettleman had given Dwyer a bad beating at Fox's American Theatre in Philadelphia. "He was good," an old-timer assured him, "maybe the best of them. Many's the time he boxed McCafferty in the gym, and took his measure, too."

From a man who had worked in Kettleman's corner as a second for several of his fights, Epperman discovered that Kettleman had once made a deal in cattle. The trail ended with a sale of four horses bearing the Six-Shooter brand.

The Six-Shooter brand, the cattle deal, the horses, the Colt pistol, all spoke of the West. Alone in his dingy office, Epperman smoked and thought, and tried to get inside Kettleman's mind. Why had he disappeared? When a man disappeared it was usually money, a woman, or both.

Kettleman had money and he had power, so it must be a woman. Yet nowhere in his investigations could Epperman turn up the slightest evidence of philandering. Before his marriage Kettleman had escorted a number of beautiful women, but was serious about none of them. Nor had he confided in any.

The trail seemed to point west but the frontier was a big place and Epperman had no desire to travel there. He had come back from a trip west only a short time before Lottie Kettleman approached him.

When Lottie arrived at the office, Epperman lighted a gas-lamp. She was a mighty fine-looking woman, but cold, Epperman thought. He had seen her kind

before—the ones who handled men the best because
they lacked passion themselves. They were always
thinking while a man was merely feeling.

"Did you know that Jim Kettleman was once a
prizefighter?" Epperman asked abruptly.

"A *prize*fighter? *Jim Kettleman?* You must be
crazy."

Epperman leaned his thick forearms on the desk
and pushed his derby to the back of his head. "He
was a fighter, all right, and a good one. Did he ever
talk about the West? Or about cattle?"

"No, not that I can remember. He talked, but it
was usually about the theater, books, politics, sometimes about horse racing."

Lottie was nettled. It was more and more obvious
that she had not learned the simplest things about the
man she had married. A prizefighter? Kettleman with
his perfect manners? It was impossible. She must
seem like a fool, not to know more about him. Now
she recalled how handsome he was, and how much
respected, and not only because of his money.

Facing it, she had to admit she was a fool. She
should have done everything to make her marriage
work, but she had been so concerned with getting information from him, trying to make a killing from
knowledge gleaned from him that she had missed her
chance. Why try to make money for herself when
Kettleman had the key to the mint?

She also confessed to herself that her respect for
him had increased tenfold since he had gone away.

Chivington came in and sat down beside his
daughter. He repeated the story, which Epperman
knew, of finding the Navy Colt in the safe. The room

began to smell of stale cigar smoke and Lottie felt her irritation mounting. Kettleman was making fools of them all.

"If I learn anything," Epperman said at last, "I'll let you know. I think," he added, "that I may have something."

Just what he had he did not know, except for a hunch that whatever it was might turn into money for them all. The first thing he must do now was to contact Porter Baldwin.

Still, if he himself could find Kettleman, maybe Kettleman would pay to stay lost. It was a thought.

All the way home he cherished the thought and developed it; at the same time a cool rational wind blew through the dark places of his brain. Kettleman had been quick to use that pistol at Saratoga, and by all accounts he was a man of decisive mind. He just might decide to use the pistol instead of paying blackmail. The more Epperman considered that possibility the more uncomfortable he became.

He was sitting on the edge of his bed rubbing his feet when he remembered the man on the train.

CHAPTER 10

DUSK CAME SLOWLY to Kaybar. From the far hills, a coyote called. A nighthawk swooped and dived in the air just overhead, and the bats were coming out. Otero loitered on his way to the stable as if to feed stock, and saddled their horses.

Thomas assured them he would be no trouble, and Flint went to Flynn's room. The foreman was barely conscious and it was foolish to move him, yet he could not be left behind.

"You don't know me," Flint said, standing over Flynn, "but I found you on the trail after you'd been shot."

"Thanks." The word was barely whispered.

"What I want to say is, we've got to move you. Shortly after dark the ranch will be attacked and they will fire the house. We have to be far from here. We're going to the Hole-in-the-Wall."

"Leave me—with a rifle. Or move me." Flynn paused to breathe deeply, and then whispered, "Stand by her ... like my own daughter."

He closed his eyes for several minutes. "Gladys. Nobody else knew I was going. She told them."

Big Julius Bent, strangely gentle for such a big man, assisted by Juana, dressed Flynn for the ride.

Nancy planned quickly and surely. Flint passed in and out of the kitchen but made no suggestion because none was needed. Food, medicines, material for bandages, blankets, canteens, matches. Only when the horses were packed and dusk was down around them did she pause to look about. "It is the only home I have ever known."

"You can build again."

"Of course." She looked at him quickly. "One does not surrender, Jim. One has to go on."

He considered that. Had he surrendered? But his death was inevitable. Or so they said. There was no cure. But people had recovered despite all the medical prophecies. Was it mental? Was it faith? Or was it some chemical within the body that could be summoned by faith or by the will?

The West held many stories of men critically wounded who had survived when thought beyond all hope.

The will to live ... it was there, and with it perhaps any disease, any illness might be defeated.

Nancy and the men moved out into greater darkness, going slowly because of the wounded. Flint remained behind with Pete Gaddis to fire a few shots and give an appearance of defense. They did not plan to remain more than a few minutes.

Lying on the veranda at a corner of the house, Flint thought how quickly a man takes on the qualities of darkness! Men who live by night, the soldier, the thief, the traveler by night, the vagabond ... theirs is a different way of thinking, and they do not fear the dark nor what may come upon them by night because they themselves are of the night, a part of it.

He had been like this long ago, and then had lost it while living in lighted places, and in comfortable surroundings. Now it was creeping into him again, becoming a part of him. He was no longer a stranger to the night, he was himself a shadow, a creeper by night, a thing to which the darkness was a comfort and a surrounding defense.

There came, off to the left, an inquiring shot. Lifting his heavy rifle, he drew a careful bead on the source of the shot, knowing if the man was an Indian fighter he would have moved by now, and he squeezed off the shot, then instantly fired to right and left. He heard a startled cry, more of alarm than pain.

Gaddis stirred. "What do you think?" he asked.

"Give them one. Then we'll go."

They moved out, walking their horses where dust lay, Gaddis using his memory of the ranch to choose the route.

Gaddis was quiet, the coyote out on the ridge was still, the bats and nighthawks were invisible now in the cloaking darkness. They were accompanied only by the hoof falls of their horses and the creak of saddle leather.

"You hunting somebody?" Gaddis asked suddenly.

Now what did that mean? Flint waited a moment before replying and then said, "No...there's nothing I want that anyone can give me."

They climbed a little, and when they were on a level again, working among the trees with only the stars listening, Flint said, "I'd like to help that girl. Believe me, I would."

They came up on the others suddenly. Far behind they heard another questioning shot. Then they saw the shadows of the bunched horses, and Flint was beside Nancy. They moved off at once.

"It is good of you to help. It isn't your fight."

"I no longer know whose fight it is. Maybe injustice is everyone's fight, now and forever."

"Who *are* you, Jim?"

He considered the question with wry humor. Who was he? A fair question, but a difficult one. He was nobody. He was a man without a name of his own, born of parents somewhere, somehow, but with no heritage of reputation, or love.

"I am nobody," he said, "I am nobody at all."

And soon he would be less than that. He would be dust—a skeleton lying in a stone house in a secret place behind the dead lava.

"You have a family?"

"I never had a family." Only a wife that wanted him dead. "There is nobody," he added, "there never has been."

"You must have friends?"

Well, the original Flint was a friend. Or was he? He did not know how Flint himself would have answered that.

"Maybe. I think I did. I believe I had one friend."

"Had?"

"He was killed. But that was long ago, and almost in another world than this."

Nancy was mystified. There was an isolation about him, an aloofness, something she could not touch. Nor was there any reaching out in him, any grasping for love. Only this strange withdrawing. She had the feeling that he shrank from getting too close to people.

Flint. Even the name had a lonely sound.

Where had he come from? What did he want?

Where was he going? Why was he here? And where was "here"?

He glanced back and saw the glow on the sky. Her eyes followed his. She drew up and watched it. "My father and uncle built that ranch with their own hands. I wonder if hope and ambition and memories and dreams catch fire, too?"

He watched the glow. "They are the intangibles. Nothing, not even fire, can destroy a dream."

A single shot sounded, then the quick reply of several rifles. She caught his arm. "Jim, one of my boys is back there."

"He's all right, believe me. And if he's not, there is nothing we could do but go back and get ourselves shot at. No." He paused, listening to the night. "Whoever it is came upon them firing the ranch. He knows you are not there or there would be shooting at the ranch, so he is just taking a few shots for himself."

"Will he get away?"

"I think so. He knows they are there, and he knows you aren't. I think he planned what he would do before he fired those shots and by now he is probably a half-mile from where he was."

Gaddis was waiting when they caught up. "You've got to know where to ride when you cross the lava," he said, "some of this solid-looking stuff is eggshell thin. Here and there you can see places where the roof of some blister has fallen in, leaving a pit nothing could climb out of."

Gaddis led the way up onto the lava. Their hoofbeats sounded like iron upon iron as they followed in single file. They went only a short distance, then descended into a hollow where there was dampness in the air and their horses rode through grass.

"The trail was smoothed long ago," Gaddis said. "Some Indian before Columbus came, probably. You have to know how to find it."

Firelight flickered on Otero's face when they dismounted. They were deep into the great twelve-thousand-acre pasture, surrounded by walls of lava nowhere less than twenty feet high.

"Do your other riders know this place?"

"Most of them. They have been with us for years, and when a man works range as long as they have, they get to know it. Also"—she gestured—"this was used to hide cattle from Utes and Apaches. The Hopi and Zuni Indians knew of the place, I think, but the raiders were always strangers."

Bent was breaking branches to make a bed for Flynn. Thomas had propped himself against a pine trunk and was building a smoke. His face looked ghastly under the leather-brown skin, but when he caught Flint's eye he winked.

"My advice is to sit tight. I'm pulling out."

Nancy turned on him. "You're leaving?"

"I want to send a telegram."

Gaddis was watching Flint make coffee. "I'd say more coffee. We like it strong."

Flint added more coffee, glancing up at Gaddis. "Something bothering you?"

Gaddis's eyes seemed to shade over. "Should there be?"

Flint got up. "Not that I know of, Gaddis."

He walked away from them toward the mare. She looked beat. She had been ridden steadily of late and she was no longer young. He made his decision then. He was going to ride the red stallion.

Sending the telegram would destroy his carefully arranged disappearance. Everyone would know where he was. But they would never know about the hideout in the lava bed. Once the land fight was over he could go there to die, as planned.

The trouble was Flint did not feel like dying. He had been warned that when his time grew near he would feel better, and there would be less pain.

He wanted to live. There lay the trouble. Before he had not cared. The prospect of death had been almost a relief after the failure of his one grasp for happiness.

The reason was obvious. Nancy Kerrigan made the difference, and even if he were to live he could not marry her.

She came to the fire just then, stretching her fingers to the warmth of the flames. "What can we do, Jim?"

He put a few drops of cold water into the coffee to settle the grounds. "Leave it to me," he said.

"What can you do against them all?"

"They aren't so many. In any such fight it is not only what you do, it is where and how you do it. An enemy has many fronts, and if one seems impregnable, attack on another."

Hoofbeats sounded and Gaddis reached a hand for his rifle. Flint faded into the shadows, waiting.

Two riders showed suddenly at the edge of the firelight. "Our boys," Gaddis said, and Flint recognized one of them as Scott. The other was introduced as Rockley. Scott was a powerfully built man who rarely smiled; Rockley, narrow-faced, with a wry twist of humor to his lips and a dry way of speaking. Both were seasoned men.

"Mornin', ma'am," Rockley said. "Nice weather for a picnic."

"How's Ed?" Scott asked.

"He stood the ride better than we expected." Nancy indicated the pot. "The coffee's fresh, hot, strong enough to float a mule shoe."

Scott walked to his horse and stripped off the saddle. As he did so he glanced at Flint, who was tightening the cinch on the mare. "Better ride Flynn's horse. Your mare's done up."

"I've another horse."

Rockley glanced at Gaddis but said nothing. He was wondering what they all were. Where did Flint keep his other horse? And who was Flint?

Flint returned to the fire for a cup of coffee, and picked up his rifle. Rockley glanced at it enviously. "That's quite a *wee*pon. You never bought that on cowhand's wages."

Flint looked over at the cowhand and smiled, realizing with surprise it was the first time he had smiled at any of them.

"I could if I robbed stages and got away with it," he said. "But that wasn't how I got it."

"No." Rockley shot him an appraising glance. "I'd not say it was."

Flint put down his cup and, with the rifle in the hollow of his arm, walked to the horse and took up the bridle. He did not look at Nancy, just started away.

"Come back soon, Jim," she said.

He walked away, making no response. How could

he promise to come back? No matter how much he might wish to return, how could he promise?

Rockley filled his cup again. "Six-Shooter brand—that's one I never heard of."

Gaddis said nothing at all, watching the rider walk away across the shimmering grass. Day had come, but he was not thinking of that. He was thinking that he liked this man, and he might have to kill him.

"I'd say that was pretty much of a man," Rockley said. "I don't know where he came from, but wherever it is they cut them wide and deep."

Scott said nothing, watching Gaddis with curious eyes.

"I'm a right curious man," Rockley said, "and I'm wondering where a man could leave a horse and be sure he was still there?"

"He said something about sending a telegram," Thomas said. "He didn't say where."

They were silent then, and they could hear Flynn's heavy breathing. If he survived this ride, it would be a miracle.

Nancy walked from the fire and stood looking after Flint. He had almost reached the path across the lava.

"Who is he?" Rockley asked.

"The name is Jim Flint," Otero replied, "He had a run-in with Nugent over east of here, and told him where to get off. One of Nugent's own men tells it.

"He had a run-in with some of the Baldwin riders out on North Plain, when he was bringing Flynn to the ranch. He killed one of Baldwin's gunhands, then he faced Baldwin down in some kind of an argument and Baldwin's hands set on him and beat him up.

"When he came out of that, he went up the street and shot the devil out of Baldwin's crew. I'd say it isn't important where he comes from or who he is as long as he's on our side."

"Now that telegram," Rockley mused. "Where could he send a telegram that would help us?"

Nobody said anything further, and the sun was up, and the fire was going out.

CHAPTER 11

JIM FLINT STUDIED the big stallion with some trepidation. The horse had become quite a pet, but how would he react under a saddle?

And how would he take to going into the tunnel?

The stallion came for the sugar and made no fuss except to jerk his head a little when the bridle was slipped on. He worked his jaws and tongue over the unfamiliar bit, and quickly accepted another chunk of sugar. When the saddle was put on he sidestepped only a little.

When the saddle was cinched tight, Flint gathered the reins, put a foot in the stirrup and swung into the saddle. The stallion took a couple of quick steps forward under the weight, and then stopped, looking around inquiringly as if to ask what Flint was doing on his back.

However, the stallion had seen the mare ridden frequently, and when Flint booted him lightly in the ribs, he walked off a few steps and stopped. When Flint booted him again, he walked off again. Flint rode him slowly around the pasture, followed excitedly by the other horses, and then Flint mounted and dismounted several times.

When Flint led him up to the tunnel, the red horse pulled back a little, but after some coaxing, came on and followed Flint through the passage.

Once outside the lava beds, Flint mounted again

and started north for McCartys, the small station east of Alamitos. The stallion stepped out fast, ears pricked and attentive.

Only two horses were tied at the tiny hitching rail before the saloon, and Flint rode directly to the station. Tying the stallion there, he looked around carefully. There was nobody in sight. He stepped into the station, a small room with a pot-bellied sheet-iron stove. Behind a half partition the telegrapher sat tipped back in his chair, reading a newspaper.

There was paper on the counter. He wrote a quick message to his Baltimore attorney. He followed it with three others, to the president of the railroad in which he was a principal stockholder, to Burroughs, and to an official of the railroad whom he himself had arranged to appoint.

The telegrapher took the messages, read them, and then looked up at Flint. He looked again at the name *"Kettleman"* signed to the messages. "What is this? Some kind of a joke?"

"It is not. Send those messages and send them now."

The telegrapher still hesitated, glancing from Flint's rough cow-country clothing to the messages. He touched his tongue to his lips. "Mister, you may be crazy for all I know. A man just doesn't come off the range and start sending telegrams like these, why it would be as much as my job is worth if . . ."

"If you don't get those wires off, and fast, you won't have any job. You'll be walking down the track wondering what hit you."

The telegrapher sat down behind his key. "And when you start sending, remember that I can read Morse as well as you can."

The telegrapher scratched his long jaw, and after a hesitant beginning, began to tap out the messages. After the first one there was a flurry of sending and then the telegrapher looked up. "The dispatcher down the line says you got to—"

"I heard him. Here is the identification."

The telegrapher glanced at the papers and then hurried back to his key.

Flint waited, smoking a cigar, while the messages were sent. All hell would break loose now. He had started the action to revoke Baldwin's right to represent the railroad in land deals of any sort at all, and with the voting power he had, he could make it stick. Once Baldwin was aware of what had been done, he would be out for blood.

Flint got into the saddle and turned the red horse down the road toward Alamitos, starting off at a fast trot.

No sooner was he out of sight than the telegrapher ran across the street to the saloon.

The two riders loafing at the bar, Saxon and Strett, were Baldwin men. The telegrapher, whose name was Haskins, did not like the riders. Earlier, they had given him a bad time and, no hand with a gun, he had pretended to ignore their ribald remarks.

Haskins stepped up to the bar. "Rye," he said. Then, winking at the bartender, he said, "You better enjoy yourselves while you can. You'll be riding the grub line in a week."

They turned on him. "What's that mean?"

"A wire just went through," Haskins said, enjoying himself, "that will revoke Baldwin's right to represent the railroad. Another wire went to a lawyer who is going to start an inquiry in Washington."

"Aah, don't give me that!"

"Wait a minute, Saxon," the other rider interrupted, "who sent those wires?"

"A man named Kettleman," Haskins said cheerfully. "James T. Kettleman!" He tossed the newspaper on the bar in front of them. On the left side of the page was a news story: *FINANCIER VANISHES!*

The second rider read it slowly, brow puckered. "Come on," he said suddenly, "Baldwin will want to know this."

"Hey!" Haskins yelled. "Gimme back my paper!"

"Go to hell!" Saxon said over his shoulder.

"Now if that's true," the bartender said, "it's going to play hob. Every train is loaded with land-hungry folks. They ain't gonna like this."

"I like it," Haskins said grimly. "You can't make me believe any honest man would have that bunch of riffraff working for him. This will be a good country when all that crowd is run out of it."

"Who will run them?" the bartender asked calmly. "Some of them will take a sight of running, seems to me."

Neither of the two Baldwin men had seen Flint, and had no reason to connect him with the telegrams. They went by him, running their horses, and he could guess what message they carried.

He rode swiftly into town and went to the office of the judge, who had refused Baldwin an order to arrest Flint.

Swinging down, he went inside. The judge recognized him at once. The mottled blue and yellow of old bruises was still on him, and there was a scarcely healed scar showing through the hair on the side of his head, below his hatbrim.

"I want to get an injunction to stop Porter Baldwin from selling any more land."

Judge Hatfield tipped back in his swivel chair and looked at Flint with shrewd eyes. "On what grounds?" he asked mildly.

"He does not represent the railroad in any sense, nor does he have title to any land in this area."

"You are sure of this?"

Flint seated himself. Briefly, he surveyed the facts of Baldwin's arrival in the vicinity and what had followed, most of which he was sure the judge already knew. Then he covered the subject of railroad and government land and the fluid condition of all land deals at the moment.

Knowing Baldwin, and knowing something of conditions here due to familiarity with the railroad land and right of way, as well as the study he had given to possible shippers of stock who might use the railroad, Flint was able to present a very lucid and concise outline of the situation.

"You understand, Mr. Flint," Hatfield said finally, "that we have no sheriff here, and no town marshal. If I issue the injunction it is highly probably it will, for the time at least, be ignored.

"As you may have discovered," Hatfield added dryly, "the letter of the law means very little out here. Conditions are fluid in more ways than one. My own presence here is due to interests in the locality although this does come within my jurisdiction."

"I understand that, sir. The injunction would remove any shadow of legality from Baldwin's actions. I doubt if even he would attempt to consummate a sale in face of an injunction."

"Might I ask what is your interest in all this?"

"It's simple enough. Porter Baldwin is making a bold attempt to push both Tom Nugent and Nancy Kerrigan off their land. They do not hold title, although both have lived upon their land for years, and have made improvements that, in the case of Miss Kerrigan, might legally constitute a title."

"I take it your interest is in Miss Kerrigan's ranch?"

"Yes."

Judge Hatfield sat up. "I will see what can be done, Mr. Flint." He got up. "You do not talk like a drifter."

"I'm not a drifter. Nor do I have any interest here in land or titles to land...except, perhaps, in railroad land. And I can assure you that within forty-eight hours there will be a wire in Porter Baldwin's hands, and a copy of it delivered to you, denying him any right to sell, lease, or in any way involve himself with railroad land."

After Flint was gone, Judge Hatfield opened his newspaper again and glanced at the item on the upper left-hand corner of the page. And then he wrote out a telegram of his own to send to the capitol in Santa Fe.

Jim Flint stood for a few minutes beside the big red horse, rubbing his neck and talking to him. It was time he returned to the Hole-in-the-Wall. He mounted and started away.

A half hour before, Saxon and Strett had reached Baldwin at the Grand Hotel.

Baldwin received the news with skepticism. "Kettleman here? Nonsense! It's a trick...or a practical joke."

Strett passed the newspaper over to Baldwin. "Take a look," he said.

Baldwin scanned the item. Kettleman was not in New York, and his wife could not be reached for comment. Peres Chivington had, however, stated that Kettleman had not seen his wife in several weeks, and that he was dead or missing.

Baldwin swore softly and strode to the window. For a minute he stood there, chewing on his cigar.

What would bring Kettleman to New Mexico? Land? Railroads? He thought swiftly. He must get copies of those wires. Despair hit him and in its wake came fury. What right had Kettleman to come barging out here and butt in? He had money enough of his own without messing up other people's plans. He paced the floor angrily, while the two gunmen waited.

Suppose . . . just suppose that Kettleman were here and were to die here? How many knew of his presence?

The telegrapher at McCartys, and these two, Saxon and Strett.

Lottie had wanted Kettleman dead, and if he died, she would inherit. If he died, opposition to Baldwin would disappear, and if he died and Baldwin knew about it, Baldwin could take advantage of the fact to make some money on the market. The news of Kettleman's death was sure to have its impact.

He must wire Lottie, and he must find Kettleman. If he was not at the hotel, where was he? Not the Kaybar, for the Kaybar was now in Baldwin's possession. Perhaps at Nugent's, or west of here at Fort Wingate.

"Go back to McCartys," he told Strett and Saxon.

"Get a description of Kettleman from that telegraph operator. And *get* it from him. I want him located, Strett. There is a hundred-dollar bonus to the man who can place Kettleman for me."

Strett took a cigar from Baldwin's desk and clipped the end with his teeth. "You want this Kettleman alive?" he asked mildly. "Or dead?"

Baldwin offered a cigar to Saxon. "I just want to know where he is," Baldwin said. "And I'd like to be sure he stays some place out of the way. The longer, the better."

"Sure," Strett agreed, "if he stayed away, say, oh, say quite a while. Mightn't that be worth a thousand dollars?"

"Five hundred."

Strett knew where he stood now. Nobody paid five hundred dollars just to have a man hidden out for a while. "He's a mighty important man," Strett replied. "I figure for a thousand dollars I could handle it. Then Saxon and me could take a trip, a real long trip."

"All right," Baldwin said, thinking of Buckdun, "that will do it. A thousand dollars."

The injunction was served, and Baldwin strangely enough made no protest. He took it quietly, and Flint, from the Hole-in-the-Wall, heard of it.

"You will be going home now," he said to Nancy.

"Home?" There was a sadness about her he had not seen before. "It will not be home again. Not yet."

She looked at him strangely. "You've a fine red horse there. And no brand. How can a horse become five or six years old and not wear a brand?"

"There are places where they don't brand at all," Flint said.

Pete Gaddis rode out that day with Johnny Otero and Julius Bent, making a swing around to check the cattle and, if it could be done without shooting, to start pushing Baldwin cattle off.

Flynn was able to sit up. Although it would be long before he was able to sit a horse again, he began handling the range once more, talking with the hands, inquiring about this place or that. Flint was around, but he did not belong somehow. There was a strangeness about them now that he could not understand. For a while they had almost accepted him.

With surprise he realized he had not spat blood for a week, and he felt better. It was time he went back to the hideout.

Yet he was worried. It was not like Baldwin to back down. Nor had he left the country. He had sold off some cattle, but he was holding the rest on Nugent range.

And then Gaddis rode in. "Nugent's dead," he said. "He was found in his own ranch yard, shot through the heart."

"Buckdun," Rockley said.

"Maybe," Gaddis said, looking over at Flint. "And maybe not."

Nancy caught the glance, and realized what it meant. Flint had said he could bring an end to it, and now Nugent was dead. There could be, she assured herself, no possible connection. Her eyes strayed to the high-powered rifle that Flint was never without these days.

Flint looked up to find their eyes on him. Slowly he

looked from one to the other. "What's the matter?" he said.

"The way I look at it," Gaddis said, "it ain't reasonable that Port Baldwin would back up like he has done, with or without that injunction. Not unless there was something he wanted done first."

"What does that mean?"

"Nugent is dead."

"So?"

"If the boss should be killed he would have a free hand, wouldn't he?"

Flint waited a full minute without speaking. The idea was one that he had never expected, never dreamed of. They believed he had killed Nugent. They believed that he intended to kill Nancy Kerrigan.

Carefully he got to his feet, rifle in hand. "What would I have to gain?" he asked them quietly. "Where could I gain anything?"

"You have a name," Gaddis said. "A name that stands for something."

Flint!

"It is not an uncommon name," he replied quietly.

"I should know," Gaddis said.

Flint was puzzled. "Look," he said, "how do you suppose that injunction was granted? It was I who went to Judge Hatfield."

"Was it?" Gaddis had faced squarely toward him now. "Flint, I say you're a liar!"

He was ready to draw, but Flint did not move. "I wouldn't try that if I were you, Gaddis. I don't want to kill you."

"Or do you mean you don't want to try when it

would be a fair shooting? Your kind pick your own spots. Well, you don't pick this one! *Draw!*"

"*No!*" Nancy spoke sharply. "Pete, stop that. There will be no gunfight here."

She turned to Flint. "I suggest you ride out of here."

He merely looked at her. "All right," he said, and walked to his horse.

Nobody spoke while he saddled up, then Gaddis said, "Ma'am, you're doing the wrong thing. I tell you he killed Nugent. It had to be him. And he's gunning for you.

"Look at it straight. When did he get here? Right after Baldwin did. Where does he go when he pulls out? Where did he get his horses? Ain't he the one had the run-in with Nugent? Tried to get him into a fight then. You heard the story."

Nancy looked across the fire at Flint's back. It was impossible, and yet she had no argument against it.

"How do we know he didn't shoot Ed himself? How do we know he didn't lead the party that attacked the ranch, and just come on in to find out where we'd go and what we'd do."

"I got a rope," Scott said.

"Hold it," Rockley said quietly, "you're going off half-cocked, Pete. We don't know any of this here. Seems to me you've got something in your craw."

Flint turned deliberately and got into his saddle. "I shouldn't have expected better of any of you," he said quietly. "The only thing I'm guilty of is making a damned fool of myself.

"Gaddis," he said, "I liked you. But you've got

something in your craw, as Rockley said it. What's wrong?"

"Flint!—that's what's wrong! Everybody knows that name! Known it for years! Why, we figured we had you at The Crossing—!

"You were there?" Flint asked mildly.

"You're damned right I was there! I was riding segundo for the Three-X! You killed our boss! Leyden spotted you in the saloon that night."

Flint was facing them all now, sitting the saddle. "And how many shots were fired into Flint while his arms were held?"

Gaddis flushed. "I—"

"His arms were held by two brave men," Flint said, "while the others shot into his body. It wasn't enough to make it nine to one, you had to hold him, too!"

Rockley was looking at Gaddis. "I never heard that part of it," he said.

"I wasn't for that," Gaddis protested angrily. "I wasn't for that, at all. Anyway, he was a dry-gulcher. He was an ambush killer."

"You shot into him how many times, Gaddis?" Flint repeated.

"How should I know? Nine or ten times . . . maybe more."

Flint reached up and, taking his shirt by the collar, ripped it from his body with one jerk. "All right, damn you," he said bitterly, "how many bullet scars do you count?"

His bare chest was white, dead white, but there were no scars, not one.

"I think, Gaddis, you've talked too damned much,"

he said. His eyes crossed the fire toward Nancy. "Believe me, ma'am, I only tried to help."

He swung the red stallion and rode swiftly away.

So he had been a fool. Now he would go back to the hideout and stay there.

If he was going to die, it should be soon.

CHAPTER 12

WHEN LOTTIE KETTLEMAN stepped down from the train to the platform at Alamitos she was no more prepared for the town than the town was for her.

Beautiful women were rare in Alamitos, and beautiful women dressed in the the very latest Paris fashions were unheard of. And Lottie's worst enemy would not deny that she was truly beautiful.

She had red-gold hair with almost violet eyes and the clear, creamy skin that one occasionally sees in truly beautiful red-haired women. Fashion had swung from the hooped skirt to dresses that moulded the figure, and Lottie Kettleman had a figure which appreciated the new styles.

Moreover, she was perfectly aware that she was entering upon a field of battle where allies were to be won and enemies defeated by what weapons she could muster, and she proposed to leave no one in doubt as to the weapons she brought to the field.

Her dress was of jersey, the new elastic cashmere fabric which offered elegance of shape and finish as well as freedom of movement. Her skirt was much narrower than anything Alamitos had seen, or for that matter, Philadelphia or San Francisco, and the polonaise of flowered material was startling.

Followed by an embarrassed young man in a dark

suit who had offered to carry her bags, Lottie crossed the street to the Grand Hotel, pausing a moment to look about her.

Alamitos had little to offer, and that little could all be seen: a few shabby buildings, the cottonwoods for which the town was named, the loafing cowhands.

What startled her was the sky. It was enormous and blue, more blue than any sky she had seen, the vast sweep of it something she could scarcely grasp.

Women stood frozen, watching her, fascinated by clothing they had seen only in *Godey's Lady's Book* or *Harper's Bazaar,* and the men were scarcely aware of the dress at all, seeing only the girl.

Lottie Kettleman swept into the lobby of the Grand and the clerk hastily swung the register toward her. "I am Mrs. Kettleman," she said. "You have a reservation, I believe?"

Within the hour she was sitting opposite Porter Baldwin in the dining room. "Where is he, Port?" she demanded.

"I wish I knew," Baldwin said irritably. "I have men looking for him, but we've had no description. I never saw him, and the telegraph operator at McCartys couldn't or wouldn't give us any adequate description."

"That's ridiculous! How many men are there in this town? If you ever see Jim Kettleman you won't forget him." She paused, debating whether to say what she had in mind, then decided against it.

Apparently nobody but the doctor and Jim knew that he was dying of cancer, and she was not planning to tell, not yet. She was sure the information would be of use.

Without seeming to do so, she studied Port Baldwin. He was a handsome man in his own brutal fashion, but uncouth. She had never cared for him.

"Leave it to me," she said, "I'll find him. Or he will find me."

She sipped her tea. "Port," she said, almost whispering, "he knows we tried to have him killed."

Baldwin was astonished. "How could he know?"

"That fool, that gambler you sent to Father. He must have talked before he died. Anyway, Jim had the Pinkertons investigating. I don't know how much he knows."

"It doesn't matter." He paused. "There's no reason why he should go back east at all. There are a lot of strange gunmen in town, and there have been half a dozen killings."

Lottie made no reply. She did not trust Port Baldwin, and whatever was done she meant to do herself.

She listened while Baldwin told her what had happened in Alamitos and of the sudden telegrams sent from McCartys by a man who signed himself Kettleman.

"When I first heard it, I didn't believe it, then I saw the paper reporting his disappearance."

"I can't understand it." Lottie was puzzled. "He is not the sort of man you pass by in a crowd. He's almost as tall as you are, and dark."

Alone in her room she sat down in the rocker near the window and tried to think out her problem. More than three months had now gone by since Jim Kettleman disappeared. Until Epperman had located the doctor and learned his diagnosis, she could think of no reason why he should disappear.

He was a strange man. Somehow he had always defeated her, even in this. She had been frightened when she realized he had discovered her complicity in the attempt to kill him. She had waited, wondering what he would do.

It was not until he had gone that she realized how much it had meant to her to be Mrs. James T. Kettleman. For the first time in her life she was somebody, she had position and money. Before that she had pretended, she had struggled to keep up appearances, she had connived and cheated.

Surprisingly, she discovered Jim Kettleman was a well-liked man. He had been aloof, in business he had been utterly ruthless, but at the same time he had been responsible for many little kindnesses of which she had known nothing.

Why had she come west? She found the question difficult to answer. If she was Jim Kettleman's widow, and inherited his money, she would be an extremely wealthy woman. But would she inherit? Burroughs had not seen the will, but he assured her that, judging by his actions, Kettleman had no intention of leaving her anything and it was highly probable that she would get little or nothing. In any event, if he disappeared, the estate could not be settled for seven years.

Disturbed, she went to the mirror and began touching up her hair. She always thought best while working on her hair.

Another woman.

The thought came to her as a shock. Somehow, she

had not thought of that, for though Jim had admired women he had never shown any inclination to seek their company.

But no. The fact that he was dying was enough reason for him to disappear. What she had to do was find him, care for him, get back in his good graces, and get him to change his will. That was reason enough for coming west.

Yet somehow she was not satisfied with this conclusion. There was something else . . . something more.

She was standing on the walk by the hotel in the late afternoon when she saw the rider on the big red horse. She was staring at him when Port Baldwin came up behind her.

"There comes that Flint," he said to her. "He has more lives than a cat, and he has caused me a lot of trouble."

"I can understand that, Port," she said. "That is James T. Kettleman!"

Porter Baldwin had believed he was beyond astonishment. Despite her words, the thought refused to register. "That's Jim Flint," he said. "He's a gunfighter."

The man on the red horse was almost up to where they stood, and he had seen her. "Hello, Jim," she said.

He walked his horse over to them. "Hello, Lottie," he said. "You're a long way from home."

"Is that all you have to say to me?"

He smiled. "Why, Lottie, I don't remember that we ever had much to say to each other." He glanced at Baldwin, amusement in his eyes. "I never saw two people who deserved each other more."

And he walked the red stallion off down the street.

"So that's Jim Kettleman . . . it isn't reasonable."

"He looks well, doesn't he?" Lottie commented. "I mean, those clothes suit him."

He *did* look well. Not like a dying man.

"Where do you suppose he's going?" she asked.

Port Baldwin took the cigar from his teeth. "Why, he's probably going to see that Kerrigan woman. She owns a ranch out south of here. She's a fine-looking girl." He relished the remark. "Real quality. Old Virginia family. Her father and uncle migrated west a long time back."

Lottie Kettleman abruptly walked away, her heels clicking on the boardwalk. Baldwin looked after her and chuckled, but he did not feel like chuckling. He went to his room, sat down on the bed with the pillows propped behind him, eased his sleeve garters, and studied the situation anew. If Kettleman and Flint were one and the same . . .

It was almost midnight before he got up and refastened his collar. The saloon was open and he wanted a drink. From the window he could hear the tin-panny piano, and a shrill soprano.

If Kettleman had sent those telegrams they would get results in New York. Baldwin's approval from the land office of the railroad company would be denied. The injunction would stand up, and his plan for a quick deal was finished. Moreover, he was holding thousands of head of cattle that represented the bulk of everything he owned. There were too many for the Nugent range with Nugent's cattle already there, and his hired gunmen were showing little interest in bucking the kind of shooting they had encountered at the Kaybar.

Kettleman, or Flint, had been the backbone of the defense at Kaybar. He had also got Hatfield to issue that injunction and thus stopped his railroad land deal.

Baldwin remembered what he had said to Lottie. The town was full of gunmen, and anything could happen.

At this moment, Saxon and Strett were hunting Kettleman. Suppose they found him and killed him?

There would still be a chance to save something here, and back east. Baldwin began going over the possibilities, trying to judge the effect Kettleman's death would have on the stocks in which he had invested. There had to be a way to make a killing.

He was not worried about talk from Strett or Saxon. He had already prepared a plan in case they did kill Kettleman, a plan that involved Buckdun. For two such drifters, Buckdun's price would be less than he must pay them if they scored on Kettleman.

Jim Flint paused at the edge of town. He had been a fool to leave the hideout, but after four quiet days he had grown suddenly restless.

He had stopped briefly at the saloon at McCartys. There the telegraph operator showed him a badly battered face and told him about Saxon and Strett. However, the town was quiet. Nugent's ranch headquarters was occupied by Baldwin men, and most of the Nugent riders were gone.

The Kaybar had pushed most of the Baldwin cattle off their range without trouble, and there was talk in town of electing a town marshal to keep the peace within the town limits.

Flint's mind kept returning to Nancy, yet he knew he was a fool. They had turned on him, with little enough to go on.

When he reached town he rode up to the Divide Saloon, left the stallion at the rail and went in. It was clean but small, with sawdust on the floor and only two tables.

Rockley, the Kaybar hand, was at the bar. With him was an older man in greasy buckskins and a battered hat.

Rockley picked up a bottle and walked to a table. The older man followed. "Join us?" Rockley asked pleasantly.

Flint came over to them. "Milt Ryan here says it was Buckdun shot Ed," Rockley said. "Milt's our wolfer at the ranch, and better than a 'Pache on a trail. He found Buckdun's tracks a few days after the shooting and trailed him to a hideout."

"Him, all right," Ryan said. "An' he leaves mighty little trail." Ryan squinted. "A feller up the street says you ain't Flint."

"Claims he knew Flint," Rockley said, "and you aren't old enough by a good many years." He gestured back up the street. "Name is Dolan...he's a bartender."

"He used to be in Abilene," Flint said.

They had a drink. Nobody talked for a while. Then Rockley said, "The boss is upset these days. Ain't like herself."

"She won't have any trouble. Before I—before I go away, I'll run Baldwin out of town."

Flint got up, and Rockley looked up at him. "If you ain't the original Flint, you got to be somebody who was there. You knew about Flint's arms being held, and that was something I never heard before."

"He was a good man," Flint said, "in his way." He had never spoken of the old killer before, and now he looked at the man in his memory. "I don't think he had any regard for human life at first. He figured he was in a war, and the cattlemen were in the right. He hated nesters. Well, he was wrong. No man is ever going to make anything right with a gun.

"Only"—he hesitated—"one time he helped a kid who needed it, and don't ask me why."

"Where did he come from? Who was he?"

"He never said. He never talked at all, come to think of it, beyond a comment about camp or the weather or when he was trying to teach me something."

Flint pulled down his hatbrim, hesitated briefly at the door and went out.

Rockley looked over at Milt Ryan. "Well, there she is, Milt. Only one person he could be, if you see it like I do."

Milt Ryan looked at his whiskey glass and at the bottle and decided against it. "He was the kid at The Crossing," he said, and got up. "Rockley, you ever see Pete Gaddis with his shirt off and his belt down low?"

"He's got a bullet scar."

"And he got it at The Crossing."

Outside in the dark street they stood together, looking carefully around.

"I been wonderin' about Gaddis," Ryan said. "He ain't been himself."

"He's got him a good memory," Rockley agreed. "He thinks Flint wants to give it to him again... higher and on the left side."

CHAPTER 13

RED DOLAN, WHO had tended bar in Dodge, Abilene, Tascosa, and Leadville among other towns, was not deceived by the quiet.

His red hair was freely sprinkled with gray, and with the passing of the wild years had come a wary appreciation of life. The frontier was in Dolan's blood. He had been tending bar the night Wild Bill Hickok killed Strawhan, and he had been hunting a job in Deadwood when Wild Bill left for Deadwood, which was to be his last town. Aside from the Army doctor who had examined Hickok, Dolan had been the only man alive who knew Wild Bill was going blind, that he barely could see the spots on his cards.

Dolan had been in Montana running a faro game when Morgan Earp killed Billy Brooks, and had known both men. He had been in Virginia City when Eldorado Johnny came up from the Colorado River country, determined to be "chief of Virginia City or the best-looking corpse in the graveyard" . . . and after Langford Peel shot him, Dolan had attended the funeral.

Red Dolan had seen them come and go, and when a youngster walked up to his bar, Dolan could almost tell within a few months how long he would last. The would-be tough ones rarely lasted long enough to have to shave more than once a week.

He had known the original Flint and had been a message center for him. Red Dolan took no sides, but if you wanted to locate a man for a job you told Red. Sooner or later the man showed up.

Old Sulphur Tom Whelan had come up from Horse Springs, and stood at the bar to share old-time talk with Red Dolan. "Buckdun and Flint," Tom said, "that's the one I want to see."

"The good ones rarely shoot it out," Dolan said, "they know even if they score they can be killed."

"They'll meet," Sulphur Tom insisted, "if Pete Gaddis doesn't tangle with Flint first."

"What's wrong with Gaddis?"

"Ask him about that scar on his belly. They do say Flint was the kid at The Crossing."

A dust devil danced in the sunlit street, and a roan horse stood three-legged at the hitch rail. A woman in a gingham dress went along the walk, holding a child by the hand. And down the street a German farmer was loading a pitchfork, shovel, and hoe into his wagon. It was a quiet day in town.

Five men loitered at the back end of the bar. All were Baldwin riders. Strett was there, and Saxon with him. At least twenty Baldwin men were in town, so the quiet did not deceive Dolan in the least.

Rumors of the telegrams sent from McCartys were getting around town. James T. Kettleman was somewhere in the country and he had thrown a monkey wrench into Baldwin's plans.

Dolan felt intimations of trouble sharpen when Rockley and Milt Ryan came in. Rockley was a salty customer. Milt Ryan was a hard-bitten old mountain man.

A few doors up the street, Jim Flint went into the Grand and, hearing familiar laughter from the dining room, he walked in. Lottie sat there with Port Baldwin, and their laughter stilled as he entered the room.

Flint nodded briefly and Lottie watched him pass. It was hard to believe that this handsome, easy-walking man was actually her husband.

Baldwin was telling her some coarse joke and she felt a flicker of irritation that she was here instead of across the room with Jim. He was one of the few men she had known who always treated her with respect.

Jim looked composed, and the lines in his face had relaxed. "I can't believe it," she said suddenly. "Jim Kettleman—a gunfighter!"

Port Baldwin looked grim. "You would have believed it the day he shot up the town. Beaten within an inch of his life, blood all over him, clothes torn, face swollen, and he scared that bunch who work for me clear out of town. He killed two men that day, and put lead into some others."

She looked at Baldwin with surprise. "You sound as if you admire him!"

"I hate his guts," Baldwin said brutally, "and I'd like him dead, but by the Lord Harry, he's a fighting man! I'll give him that. He's a real fighting man."

He gulped coffee, put the cup down, and then added, "With a gun, he is. I'd give a-plenty to get at him with my hands. I'd like to pound his face in."

"You couldn't do it, Port, so don't ever try." Lottie surprised herself by the comment.

He looked at her in obvious astonishment. "I *couldn't*? Are you crazy?" He doubled a ham-like fist. "I could beat him to death with this. Nobody ever stood up to me in a fist fight, nor rough and tumble, either."

He opened his big right hand. "I can bend sixty-penny spikes like you fold a newspaper." He indicated Flint. "I'd break him like he was a dry stick."

Lottie regarded him coolly. "Don't ever try it, Port. I have a feeling that we had better leave him alone. He's poison for us. Bad luck."

"Not if he's dead."

Lottie glanced down the room at Flint. He did not look like a man who was dying. But what if he did die? What if he died now, where everybody would know he was dead? A good lawyer—and then all those millions, in Paris, Vienna, London.

"I must talk to him. That is why I came out here, you know."

Coolly, as she listened with half her attention to Port Baldwin, her thoughts sorted out the situation. It might require several long fights in court, but no matter what sort of a will he had left, she was sure she would win in the end.

To get that money Jim had to be dead. There was no sense in letting her head be turned by the fact that he was attractive. Men were attractive to her only insofar as they could supply her with what she wanted. She wanted money, she wanted the attention of men, and she wanted to control men.

"You're a fool if you think you can get anywhere by talking," Baldwin said, "because he will not listen, and it will not matter whether he does or not."

She drew back her chair and got to her feet. "Nevertheless, *I* shall talk to him."

She went down the room to his table with every

eye upon her, and when she reached him he got to his feet and drew back a chair for her. "Will you sit down, Lottie? I am sure you will understand if I do not say I am glad to see you."

When she was seated she said quickly, "Jim, you should have stayed in New York. You can have better care."

"So he told you, did he? I fancied he was an old gossip. I was a fool to have gone to him."

"He is the best doctor in New York!"

"The most fashionable, you mean. It does not follow that he is also the best."

"Are you coming back?"

"Of course not."

"Jim . . . what about me? You spoiled me, Jim. I can't live on a hundred dollars a month."

He looked up at her, coldly amused. "I am sure you can if you must. But I did not expect you to. I expected you would find someone else, marry him, and that someone would, of course, be able to support you in the style you believe you deserve."

"What makes you think I want to marry again?"

"Lottie, you never wanted to marry. It was merely a device. You will marry again, but you will not want to. It is simply the easiest way for you to get the things you want."

"There's another girl?"

"When I may have only a few weeks—perhaps a few days? I have already gone past the time I was expected to live, I believe. No, there is no other girl."

There was Nancy Kerrigan. His thoughts returned to her, and the way she had looked at him. Her cool, steady gaze had reached some longing deep within him, secret even from himself.

Too many things were secret even from himself, for, once he examined them in the cold light of day, he would know they were not for him. Nothing in his life had geared him for love, for a home, for the life other men led. His was a lonely way, and instinctively he had avoided all thought along such lines, living and dealing on the surface and with surface values.

With such a girl as Nancy . . . but why think of that? He had been ordered to leave, despised by her and by the others.

Pete Gaddis he had liked. Looking at that, he realized he still liked the man. There was something there . . . of course it was that old affair at The Crossing.

But The Crossing was years ago and far away. The dead had long been buried. The old feelings were gone. Flint was dust, but he had been avenged before he died. In the old Viking way, enemies had been buried to go with him to whatever hunting grounds remained for one like Flint.

Lottie was irritated. For the first time in her life she was sitting with a man and his attention was wandering. With a kind of desperation she realized that Jim Kettleman, or Flint, or whatever his name was, had slipped away from her and she simply was not going to get him back.

"I wasn't much of a wife to you, was I, Jim?"

"No, you weren't." He looked across the table at her gravely. Beautiful? Yes, she was beautiful, but with no sense of good or evil except as it was good or evil for her.

"I am riding out of town in a little while, and I am not coming back."

She fought down her anger and frustration, knowing it would defeat her purpose now. "Where will you go?"

"I think you know where I am going, and I have to go alone."

"But until then? Jim, you can't leave me like this! Why—why, I have scarcely money enough to get home!"

He looked at her and felt no compassion. They were less than strangers. She had tried to have him killed and, he was sure, would try again. And blame him for the necessity.

"I went away because I wanted to die alone, as I have lived, and that is what I shall do."

He pushed back from the table and her anger destroyed her judgment. "It's that Kerrigan girl! That was why you interfered with Port! That cheap little ranch girl!"

He smiled at her. "Lottie, she is neither cheap, nor exactly little, and she is something you will never be—a lady. You have the appearance, she has the quality and the heart. Yes, if things were different, if I had a few years to live and she would have me—but why talk foolishness?"

He got to his feet and took up his hat. Lottie started to speak, but suddenly she was empty of words. With what could you threaten a man who was dying and prepared to die?

They were alone in the room now.

"I'm glad you're dying." She looked up at him and he thought he had never seen such concentrated hatred in the eyes of anyone. "I'm really glad. And when you die, I hope you think of me, because I'll be *alive*!"

Her lovely mouth was twisted with fury, but all he felt was relief. "Lottie, you're your own worst enemy. The quiet, simple little girls will end up with all the things you want, and you'll be conniving, cheating, and baiting hooks until you're old and broke and empty. Believe me, you have my sympathy."

He walked out into the night.

On the walk he paused. A rider was coming along the quiet street, a tall man on a horse that walked steadily forward. The legs of the horse showed, then the splash of white on his chest, and then both animal and rider came into the light at once.

Buckdun.

If the gunman saw Flint standing on the boardwalk, he gave no indication, but walked his horse on past, holding the reins in his left hand, eyes straight before him.

There was no nonsense about Buckdun. He used a gun because he was good with a gun, and he avoided trouble because trouble led to more trouble and there was no money in it.

Once in Silver City, Flint had heard, a man called Buckdun a liar. Buckdun looked at him coolly and said, "You may think what you like," and turned his back.

Frustrated, the would-be gunman stood looking around angrily, helplessly.

Furious, he shouted, "I can beat you to the draw! I am faster than you!"

Bored, Buckdun looked at him in the mirror and said, "All right, you're faster than I am."

Somebody laughed and the gunman turned sharply, but saw only sober faces. Buckdun lifted his beer and took a swallow and, after a few minutes, the would-be gunman walked out.

Port Baldwin was sitting on his bed in the dark bedroom when Buckdun came in. Baldwin took the cigar from his mouth and poked several bills toward Buckdun. Buckdun picked them up and, after a glance, pocketed them.

"Flint," Baldwin said, "and I will double the ante."

"No."

"May I ask why?"

"He's too smart, and he has no pattern."

"Pattern?"

"Of living," Buckdun replied impatiently. "He isn't fixed anywhere, he doesn't belong anywhere, you can't count on his being any particular place. A man who works somewhere, lives somewhere, has friends he visits or who owns something—they are the easy ones. But Flint is without a pattern. Such men are difficult and they are dangerous."

"Three thousand."

"No. Not for any price. Why should I? I play it safe, I do very well. In a few years I shall retire and I'll have enough for my own outfit, far from here."

Baldwin rubbed out his cigar. He was angry, and he was worried. Saxon and Strett had done nothing, and he was afraid they would do nothing. And Flint had to die.

It was a matter of first importance now, for with Flint dead, it would be a simple matter to get his deal with the railroad working again. Old Chivington could influence Lottie into helping and they could, between them, come off with something.

But Flint must die... even if Baldwin killed him himself.

CHAPTER 14

NO ONE IN Alamitos doubted that trouble was impending. Red Dolan polished glasses with a wary eye on the five Baldwin riders. At the front of the bar Milt Ryan and Rockley stood talking in low tones, occasionally drinking. Milt had hunted wolves and mountain lions so long he had taken on some of their characteristics. Rockley was not one to sidestep a difficulty. All the ingredients were present but one, and that was supplied by the arrival of Pete Gaddis. Until then the Baldwin men had not identified Ryan and Rockley.

Down the street in front of Doc McGinnis's office, Julius Bent considered the situation. A big, serious man, known for his unfailing good nature as well as his great strength, Bent had come to town with Nancy and the others.

Nancy had gone to the hotel for supper. Should he go there and stand by in case she needed him, or should he get the boys together and be ready to leave?

Scott and Otero were at the store loading a buckboard with supplies, and few of the townspeople were visible. Julius Bent realized the situation was explosive.

When Nancy Kerrigan entered the dining room of the Grand the only person present was a beautiful girl with red-gold hair, dressed in the height of fashion.

Faintly curious, Nancy glanced at her and was startled to find the girl staring at her with undisguised hostility.

The waitress came to Nancy for her order and called her by name, for Nancy had been coming to the Grand from the day it opened. When the waitress started for the kitchen, Lottie got to her feet and approached the table.

"Miss Kerrigan, is it? I am Lottie Kettleman."

"How do you do? Would you like to sit down? It is rather lonely eating by oneself."

Lottie seated herself and studied Nancy with shrewd, appraising eyes.

Puzzled, Nancy tried to make conversation. "Have you been in Alamitos long?"

"Are you trying to be funny?"

"No." Nancy replied coolly. "What is it you want?"

"I said I was Lottie Kettleman." She paused. "I am the wife of James T. Kettleman."

"No doubt that is very important, but I am afraid I do not understand what it is you want?"

Lottie was growing angry, but at the same time she began to doubt if what she had suspected were true. Nancy Kerrigan was obviously puzzled.

"You know my husband, I believe. In fact, you have been spending a good deal of time together."

"You are mistaken. I devote my time to my ranch, and I have almost no social life. I do not know any James T. Kettleman."

"But you know a Jim Flint."

Nancy stiffened ever so slightly. "Of course. I believe everyone in Alamitos at least knows who he is. He has—shall I say, he has attracted attention?

Several times he has been concerned with ranch business. That is all I know of him."

"You mean you didn't know that Jim Flint was James T. Kettleman?"

"I am sure I did not. I am also sure that it would make no difference to me. One name is as unfamiliar as the other."

Suddenly she remembered the stories about the presence of Kettleman in the area, the telegrams Flint had sent, the sudden ending of Baldwin's franchise to handle railroad land. "Do you mean to say," she asked, deeply astonished, "that Jim Flint is *that* Kettleman? The financier?"

"And my husband."

Nancy turned her eyes on Lottie Kettleman. Jim... married. And to this woman.

She was beautiful, but hard. Shallow, too, if Nancy was any judge. Apparently Lottie believed there was something between herself and Jim Flint.

And was there?

For a moment she looked back...there had been something. Was it unspoken understanding? No word of love had passed between them. And then finally he had left, suspected by some of her hands of being the man who shot Ed Flynn.

"I am sure," she said quietly, "that is very interesting. I had no idea that Jim Flint was anything but what he appeared to be, and I cannot see how it can be any concern of mine. Either that he is James Kettleman or that he is your husband."

Somehow she had never thought of Jim as a married man. It was true that he had made no advances, but she had been sure of his interest, and...yes, she had been interested. For the first time in her life she had found a man who really excited and interested her.

But why was he here? What would such a man be doing in New Mexico, riding the range, engaging in gun battles, and leading a seemingly pointless existence?

"I cannot imagine what James Kettleman would be doing in Alamitos. Or why he would come here alone, if you were his wife."

Lottie Kettleman did not like being on the defensive. She did not like being called upon to explain her position, and it angered her that this ranch girl should be so poised and sure of herself.

She could not believe that Nancy Kerrigan had not known who Jim Flint was, yet Nancy's tone was sincere, and she was obviously surprised. Also, the suggestion from Lottie that there might have been something between them had aroused no reaction.

"I can tell you what he is doing here," Lottie said suddenly. "He came here to die."

Nancy looked at her but for several seconds the meaning did not register. "To die? You mean, to get himself killed?"

"To die." Lottie felt malicious pleasure in repeating it. If this girl had been getting cozy with Jim, she might as well know it would do her no good. "He's going to die. He has cancer."

Nancy looked across the table at Lottie, and for a moment her mind was blank with incomprehension. "Cancer? *Jim?*"

"Jim, is it? And you scarcely knew the man?" Lottie smiled across the table at her. "I think you're in love with him, and a lot of good it will do you. If he lives he is mine, and if he dies, you can have him."

Jim . . . he was dying then. He had reason not to care about being killed. She remembered the staggering, beaten man who had gone up the street, gun in hand, smashing into saloons, shooting, shouting, fighting. A man half blind with pain, but driven by a kind of wild desperation such as she had never seen.

Nancy no longer thought of the girl across the table. She no longer cared that only a few hours ago she had dismissed him from her camp at the Hole-in-the-Wall. Hours? Or was it days?

He was ill . . . he was dying . . . and he was alone.

She looked across the table at Lottie. "If that is true, your place is with him. He will need help, comfort, nursing, and attention."

"Let him die." Lottie got to her feet. This whole meeting had been ill-advised and had come to nothing. She was angry with herself, but more angry with Jim, blaming him for her wasted time and effort. "He is a cold, hard man. He came out here just to keep anyone from knowing when he died or where his body was. Just so he could keep me from getting what is mine."

"Go to him," Nancy said. "You are his wife. Go to him and help him. It is not an easy thing to die alone."

"You are the one interested. You go." Lottie walked to the street, filled with futile anger.

There was nothing she could get hold of, and she felt she was losing out. Jim would die and she would have nothing and would once more go back to dodging the landlord, cadging meals from men who drank

172 / Louis L'Amour

too much and just wanted to put their hands on her. Jim had given her a taste of good living, of living without worry, and now he was slipping away.

She had no thought of failure herself, at least no thought of failing as a wife. She did not want to be a wife, now or ever. She did not want to be dependent. She wanted to have the money without the strings attached. And she had her chance in Jim...if he should die or be killed now, here, where he could be seen.

From down the street sounded a tin-panny piano, and suddenly she saw Jim, angling across the street in the dark. She would know his walk anywhere. She felt the weight of her purse where her gun lay. She was a fair shot and he was not far-off and if she shot him now there was small chance she would ever be suspected...not with the enemies he had.

She put her hand in her purse and felt the cold steel of the pistol. She looked down the street and saw Jim walking up the opposite side, but toward her.

He seemed unconscious of her presence, and she drew the pistol from her bag, mentally judging the distance. Suddenly the hotel door opened and Nancy Kerrigan came out.

Quickly she put the pistol back into the purse and saw Nancy's eyes upon her.

"You might miss," Nancy said. "The dark can be deceiving. And if you missed...what then?"

"I don't know what you're talking about."

"A man like Jim," Nancy said, "if he is shot at will shoot back. It is instinctive. You could be killed."

She would not have fired, anyway. It was purely

the impulse of the moment, and her own desperate need.

Lottie turned sharply away and walked down the street, her heels clicking on the walk. She had little cash. She would return to New York with only a check for one hundred dollars awaiting her and bills for twenty times that much. There were jewels she could sell, although precious few of them, and then she would be back to the old hand-to-mouth living with her father's complaints in her ears.

Suppose she followed Jim down the street, told him she loved him, begged to take care of him? It would not work. She could not do it well and Jim was past believing anything she could say.

There was another way. There was that man of whom she had heard since coming to town. There was Buckdun.

She turned to look after Jim, but he had disappeared.

Suddenly from the shadows near the hotel, not thirty feet away, Buckdun emerged. She caught a glimpse of his narrow, pock-marked face in the light from the hotel window. She started toward him when, from down the street, there was a swift cannonade of gunfire.

Buckdun seemed to merge with the awning post and a tied horse, lean, towering, and waiting.

The gunfire burst briefly again. For an instant there was silence, and then the swinging doors of the Divide Saloon opened and a man lurched out, fell against the hitch rail, rolled around with his shoulder on the rail, and then fell off into the dust. He started to rise, and another man stepped into the doorway and fired, a cool, carefully aimed shot.

Buckdun stood for an instant, then glanced at her, and started toward his horse. He had his foot in the stirrup when she said, "Buckdun! Wait...I want to talk to you."

CHAPTER 15

JULIUS BENT, WALKING toward the Divide Saloon when the sudden thunder of guns broke the stillness, was the sole witness to the stopping of Buckdun by Lottie.

The gunfire could mean but one thing. Kaybar was in trouble, and he noticed the meeting simply because it was in his line of vision and because Buckdun was a factor in the range war.

In the brief minutes before the outbreak of shooting, Baldwin had entered the saloon, then left, followed by Strett and Saxon. Three other Baldwin riders had gone in.

Julius Bent had not witnessed a brief conversation between Baldwin, Strett, and Saxon. "Flint has gone down the street. There'll be a fight inside, and when it starts, he'll come running. Pick your spots and get him when he comes up the street. He'll never know what hit him."

Dolan had seen Sandoval come in, and Alcott with him. Sandoval was wanted in Texas and Sonora, a cool, dangerous man. Alcott was poisonous as a rattler.

"Pete," Dolan said under his breath, "for God's sake, get your boys out of here. That's Sandoval—and Alcott."

Scott and Otero had come in, and there were now

five Kaybar riders and seven Baldwin men. "Let's go," Gaddis said, to Milt Ryan, "the boss will be ready to go."

"You go if you want," Ryan said, "I ain't a-gonna miss this."

Gaddis saw that Milt was carrying his Winchester carbine. It hung by the sling from his shoulder, under the knee-length coat, muzzle down, trigger guard to the fore.

A dozen times Gaddis had seen Ryan shoot from that position, whipping the barrel up with his right hand, grasping it with the left and firing from the hip faster than most men could draw a pistol.

It was Alcott who started it. He was a lean young-ster with a wolfish face above a scrawny neck that emerged from a collarless shirt. "Ain't much of a man," he said, "who'll work for a lady boss."

Sandoval had been watching Milt Ryan. The old wolfer was the man he feared.

As Alcott spoke, the Kaybar riders swung from the bar and a scar-faced kid among the Baldwin riders grabbed for a gun. Ryan's carbine leaped from be-neath his coat, and the shot caught the kid in the belly. He screamed and jumped back, butting into the table which slid along the floor.

It was pure accident that the table slid, but it was to make all the difference.

The scar-faced kid failed to get a shot off and the table staggered two men at the crucial instant. Gaddis got off two fast shots at a range of six feet and saw two men falling, one's gun going off into the floor. Ryan's Winchester was firing as fast as he could work the lever.

Alcott had stepped behind the corner of the bar, and in the split second it took for Ryan to fire and the table to slide, Alcott saw he was a dead man if he stayed. Turning he threw both arms across his face and dove through the window, glass and all. He lit on his knees and came up running.

With Ryan's man down, Alcott gone, and two men down from Gaddis's bullets the Kaybar men centered their fire on the three remaining. One of them, Sandoval, was already falling from Ryan's fire.

As suddenly as it had begun, it was over, and the Kaybar riders stared at one another, amazed by their good luck. The shooting had lasted no more than ten seconds, and not one of them was scratched.

"Let's finish the job," Ryan said. "There's still Baldwin men in town."

One of the men Gaddis had shot tried to rise. "Call a doc!" he said. "I'm hit bad!"

"He's right down the street," Ryan said. "Get him yourself."

As one man they started for the door.

Flint had not come running, contrary to Baldwin's expectations. He heard the gunfire from the office of Doc McGinnis, where the old Army doctor, veteran of the Civil and Indian wars, had started a checkup.

Doc McGinnis stared at Flint through hard old eyes. "What's the matter with you?"

"I've got cancer."

McGinnis put down his pipe. "You have, have you? Now, who told you that?"

"Dr. Culberton...Manning Culberton of New York. I don't suppose you've heard of him."

"You could be wrong, young man. I've heard of

him, all right. Plays wet nurse to a lot of chair-polishers...one himself. I don't think he'd know a cancer from a fistula or a broken arm from a sore throat. He's been treating people for imaginary illnesses so long he wouldn't know what to do if he came bang up against something big. Cancer, eh? You lost any weight?"

"I've gained a little."

"Tell me about it."

Flint described his symptoms and what Dr. Culberton had said, as well as how he had felt then and now.

McGinnis checked him over carefully, asked a few more questions, then said dryly, "You've no more cancer than I have. What you seem to have is ulcers." He walked to his desk. "You're Kettleman, aren't you? Heard you were in town. Ulcers a common thing for men in your business. Too busy, too tense, too much worry, wrong meals at the wrong times."

McGinnis seated himself on the corner of his desk. "Losing weight at the start, that's to be expected. From what I hear you haven't been living a sensible life for a man with ulcers. What you need is rest, sleep, and lack of worry."

Flint smiled. "Doctor, I've had more rest and sleep and less worry since I've been out here than ever before. I've eaten very little but beef or beef broth, and that almost without any seasoning because I didn't have it."

"Seems to me you've had plenty to worry about," McGinnis said ironically. "You mean to say all that fighting didn't worry you?"

"How could it? Nothing was at stake but my life and I thought that was already gone."

"You can start worrying then, because I think you're going to live. Fact is, I'd say you were strong as a mule right now. Most likely all you needed was fresh air, rest, and freedom from all that hassle." He stuffed his pipe. "Water might help, too. Lots of alkali in some of it. Anyway, I'd say you were a lot better than when you came here, judging by what you've said."

He put the pipe in his teeth. "Nancy had me to see you after that beating, as you'll recall. Fine girl... known her since she was a child."

Flint was buttoning his shirt and suddenly his fingers stopped and he stared at the wall.

He was not going to die. He was going to live.

To live... and he was a married man.

"I should have met her a few years ago," Flint said, "I'm a married man... a very sadly married man."

"I've seen her. Quite a filly."

Heavy boots sounded on the steps outside. Flint picked up his gun belt and stepped back into the deeper shadows. The other gun he held in his hand.

Outside the floor boards creaked and a shadow showed on the curtain. Doc McGinnis had seated himself and was at work on a ledger, as if alone. Flint waited, holding his breath and watching the door knob, expecting it to turn.

The boards creaked again, gravel scuffed, and then the gate creaked. Whoever it had been, he was gone.

"You know something, Doc? I think I was scared."

"You've got something to lose, boy. Must be something to feel like you've been... like you were immune

to everything. Knowing it was coming, you'd nothing
to worry about."

McGinnis sucked at his pipe. "Struck me Nancy
set store by you, son. Are you sure that wife of yours
don't want you back?"

"She never wanted any man except as a setting,
Doc. She wanted money, prestige, and the attention
of men, but she didn't want marriage. She tried to
have me killed, and I believe she will try again."

"There's divorce. Folks frown on it, but I'd say it
was the only answer for some. I'd like to see Nancy
happy."

"So would I." Flint thrust the gun into his waistband "How much do I owe you, Doc?"

"Two dollars. There's a back way out if you want
to take it."

"I'm not that scared. I'll go the way I came."

There was a chill wind off the Continental Divide,
but a mockingbird sang its endless songs in a cottonwood tree. It was very late. Only a few lights showed:
the Grand Hotel, the Divide Saloon, and the livery
stable where he had left Big Red.

One light showed on the second floor of the
Grand. That would be Lottie. She always hated to go
to bed, and never wanted to get up.

He could see only the lighted window. Inside Lottie
sat in a straight chair and across from her, in the
rocker, was Buckdun.

He held his hat in his hand, his blond hair plas-
tered tight against his long skull, his wind-honed face
sharp under the light.

Lottie had never seen a man who looked so clearly

what he was. The narrow face, the eyes that had no depth, the thin lips and the gash that was his mouth.

"Buckdun," Lottie said, "I want you to do something for me."

He was looking at her as if he had never seen a woman before. And he never had—not, at least, a woman like this.

CHAPTER 16

FLINT'S BOOT HEELS sounded on the gravel, and there was no other sound. Several miles to the south the Kaybar riders headed for the Hole-in-the-Wall.

In the Divide Saloon, Red Dolan cleaned up after the fight. Wearily, he swept up the bloody sawdust, and carted the dead men out to the barn to be buried the next morning.

Seated on his bed in the darkness, Porter Baldwin smoked and waited for Strett and Saxon. But even as he waited for the news that would mean victory, and might mean wealth, he felt regret. Kettleman, or Flint, he was too good a man to go out from a gunshot in the night.

He was a fighter, and it would have been a real pleasure to whip him with fists. It had been a long time since Baldwin found anyone to stand up to him for more than a minute. To Port Baldwin there were few pleasures greater than a good fight, and Kettleman might have given it to him.

Yet, as nothing happened, he grew impatient. The trap must have failed. Baldwin smoked and waited, becoming increasingly irritable.

Flint reached the livery stable but paused at the corner of the building in deep shadow. There was a light over the huge door, and no one in sight, but inside it was a cavern of darkness, and he liked none of it.

He waited for several minutes, but heard no sound from within beyond an occasional snore from the hostler who slept in the small office at one side of the door. Finally, unable to rid himself of his apprehension, he turned and walked back to the rear of the building where the corrals were.

There, at the corral, he waited. The night was moonless, but his eyes could make out the corral bars, horses standing in the far corral, the gleam of water in a trough, and the bulk of a couple of huge freight wagons standing in the yard near the corral.

There was a back door to the livery stable also, and to this he made his way.

His feet made no sound here for the old corral was soft with dust, hay, old manure, and straw. Near the wall of the building he paused, listening again.

Far-off, back in the trees near Doc McGinnis's house, the mockingbird was still singing, but the distant sound seemed only to emphasize the stillness. In his mind he traced the steps he must take to where the red stallion waited, and it was almost halfway along toward the front door of the big barn.

The door near which he stood was as wide as that in front for the passage of hayracks and other large wagons, but it was in complete darkness. Flint waited a minute longer and then stepped inside the barn.

His feet made a soft rustle in spilled hay. He stood near the wall, waiting for a reaction, and there was none.

He could hear horses munching grain, and occasionally one stamped or blew. Otherwise the stillness was complete. There was the smell of fresh hay, of manure, and of leather. Living with danger had sharpened his senses, and he was uneasy without having justification for it.

He took two careful steps, then another. He was probably being a fool. There was no one here, and perhaps nobody wanted to kill him now. Yet Port Baldwin was still in town, and Lottie was here . . . and he had no reason to trust Lottie.

He took several quick, careful steps, then stopped. Suddenly, from within a few feet he heard a deep sigh.

Something brushed lightly at his shoulder and putting his hand up he touched a bit. It was removed from its bridle and hanging from a nail, and felt rusted and old. With careful fingers, to make no sound, he eased the bit from the nail, and judging the location from which the sigh had come, he drew back his hand and threw the bit, threw it waist high and hard, for he thought the man was sitting down.

The bit thudded against something and a voice demanded, "You tryin' to be funny? What the hell is the idea?"

"Shut up, will you?" said a second voice.

"Well, stop throwin' things! This ain't no time for horsing around."

There was a moment of silence and then the second voice said, "I didn't throw anything."

The silence was deeper.

Now they would be worried. They would be listening intently, staring all around. Crouching, careful to make no sound, Flint felt through the layers of hay and straw on the ground and got a handful of sand.

If he threw sand at the man he had struck with the

bit, he might get it in the man's eyes. If his eyes were averted and some sand struck him, he would quickly look around. It was simple as that.

Flint swung his hand wide, allowing some of the sand to escape between his thumb and forefinger. There was a sharply drawn breath and he threw the rest. He heard a gasp, and the rustle of clothing and he stepped around the stall.

One hand dropped swiftly, feeling for the target, and when his hand touched the crouching man's shoulder, the gun barrel followed. He struck with a thud, and the man grunted and fell against the stall. Flint caught him by the collar and struck him again.

Then heaving the man erect, he shoved him, with all the strength he had, toward the stall from which he had heard the other voice.

"Sax! What the—?"

Saxon lay sprawled in the center of the barn, dimly visible in the light from the big front door. Strett whispered hoarsely, but Saxon lay still. Strett had heard a rustling of clothes, a faint rattle, a thud. Had Saxon been kicked?

He waited an instant, then emerged from the stall and crouched beside Saxon. "Sax . . . what's the matter? You hurt?"

In the silence, Strett heard the click of a cocked pistol and froze, his heart pounding heavily. He was crouched down, his coat over the butt of his pistol. Swiftly he gauged his chances and decided he did not like them.

"You pick up your partner," Flint said, "and walk out of the door. Walk slow and keep both hands on him. I don't want to kill you, but on the other hand, I wouldn't mind. You make your own choice."

Strett got to his feet, slung Saxon over his shoulder, and started out.

Flint stepped quickly into the stallion's stall and spoke softly to him. Watching across the stallion's back, Flint adjusted the girth and slipped on the bridle, then he led the stallion out and stepped into the saddle.

Strett had stopped just outside the door. Flint rode up behind him and, leaning down, took his pistol from its holster, then took the gun from Saxon.

"Walk up the street," he said, "and keep going. Head for California."

"California!" Strett protested. "Can't we get our horses? Look—!"

"After I am gone, you can get your horses if you feel lucky. But if I were you, I'd get into the saddle and ride. From what I hear that's a coming country out there, and neither of you boys have any future here.

"My name is Flint, and when I see either of you again, I'm going to start shooting . . . no matter where it is. And you have had all the warning you are going to get."

He watched Strett staggering up the street under his burden, and then he rode away.

The near mountains loomed black, a cool wind blew from the pines on the high slopes. He turned south, forded the trickle of the San Jose, and took the trail to the hideout.

In his darkened room at the Grand Hotel, Porter

Baldwin at last snubbed out his cigar. So they had failed him. Flint was still alive.

Baldwin pulled off his shirt and pants, rolled into bed in his long underwear, and lay staring up at the ceiling. He could not hold his cattle on that Nugent grass forever. Already it was overgrazed and would start losing weight, yet to sell now meant a loss and the added risk of losing the cost of shipping to the eastern market.

Somewhere down the hall a door closed softly. Baldwin listened. No footsteps passed his door, but after a moment he heard a sound from the head of the back stairs, and a faint creak of a boot on a step.

Somebody was going down the back stairs! Somebody who left the hotel after midnight. Who used the back stairs? Possibly many people, but he knew of only one. Buckdun. Lottie's room was down the hall, and Lottie was anxious for Flint to die. Baldwin turned on his side and stared at the window, and was like that when he went to sleep.

Miles away to the south, at the Hole-in-the-Wall, Nancy Kerrigan was not asleep. She had been lying awake for some time when she got up and threw wood on the fire and seated herself, wrapped in a heavy coat, on a log near the flames.

Jim was dying. He was dying somewhere, and he was alone. So many things began to shape to a pattern now. Staring into the flames, she saw his face there. She poked at the fire, remembering Lottie Kettleman. She was cold, but she was lovely, and it was obvious she knew how to please men.

If Jim was dying, and Lottie hated him, why was she here?

Money. . . .

Did Jim have money? Of course. He was James T.
Kettleman, numbered among the richest men in the
country, along with Vanderbilt, Gould, Fisk, and
young Harriman. Of course he had money. If he died,
then Lottie would have it all, so why was she here?
There were so many puzzles . . . his connection with
Flint, if there was one. Yet a wire from him had been
enough to destroy the land empire that Baldwin had
been about to build.

All that was unimportant. The important thing
was that Jim was out in the hills somewhere, dying.
She remembered him lying in the guest room at the
ranch, his face horribly bruised from the beating, and
she remembered the way he had ridden from here,
practically driven from the Hole-in-the-Wall after he
had done so much.

She heard a light step and looked up to see Pete
Gaddis coming to the fire.

"Something wrong, ma'am?"

"I was thinking about Jim Flint."

Pete Gaddis hunkered down near the fire. "I was a
damn' fool. All I could think of was that he had come
hunting me, after all these years."

Nancy told Pete of her talk with Lottie. She told
him about the cancer, and she told him about Lottie.

"I'm sorry, ma'am. I surely am."

She stayed by the fire alone. There was a restless-
ness in her that denied sleep, and there was anger in
her, too, anger that a woman such as Lottie Kettleman
had married Jim.

She had no right to him . . . none at all.

But she did. She was married to him, and no matter what happened to Jim, she would still be married to him.

Nancy Kerrigan got to her feet and looked off at the faint lightening of the sky in the east. No matter...if Jim Flint was going to die he would die among those who cared for him. And she was going back to the Kaybar headquarters and build again, and if Porter Baldwin wanted trouble, he would get it.

And if Lottie Kettleman wanted Jim Flint, she would have to fight for him.

CHAPTER 17

THE MALPAIS, THAT dreaded death trap of lava, lay still and hot under the afternoon sun, and upon its vast and rugged expanse, nothing moved. From the edge of the mesa, Buckdun studied the malpais with careful eyes.

Three days had passed since the fight in the Divide Saloon at Alamitos, a fight that ended disastrously for the Baldwin riders. Three days since the night he had talked to Lottie Kettleman.

In those three days Buckdun, a cautious and relentless manhunter, had been tracking the man he was to kill.

As he had previously told Baldwin, a man with no fixed habitation or habit is most difficult to kill, for the simple reason there is no place where one may lie in wait.

Flint came from nowhere and vanished into nowhere.

Yet he had to have a hideout, and the two horses with which he had been seen had to be kept somewhere. Moreover, the red stallion wore no brand, which indicated it had been a wild horse. And such a horse had been seen on no range, for no cowhand was apt to forget such a fine stallion.

Seated upon the mesa, hidden among the trees and rocks, Buckdun assembled what information he had.

Flint had appeared at Horse Springs. His gun battle with the Baldwin riders had taken place on North Plain while riding north. He had come to Alamitos several days later from the south.

He had been involved in the fighting at the attack on the Kaybar, and had been seen riding to that ranch ahead of the attackers and coming from the south. He had visited the telegraph station at McCartys. Most of his visits to Alamitos had brought him to town from the south or east.

That indicated a hideout somewhere south or east of Alamitos and north of Horse Springs.

The implication was obvious. Flint's hideout must have been somewhere in the malpais or around Ceboletta Mesa. Nonetheless, Buckdun had drifted south and west. He had checked the old Indian ruins near Post Office Flat and Old Redondo Canyon. He had ridden along both sides of the Zuni Range.

He checked the tracks left by the red stallion. The shoes were new and distinctive. He found no such tracks anywhere west of the Kaybar. He picked up a trail several days old south of Kaybar and backtrailed it to North Plain, where it faded out. His time was not wasted, for he had learned a little. He picked up a fragment of trail headed south toward Horse Springs, a very old trail, mostly blown out by wind.

He narrowed his wide circle, and soon had decided the hideout had to be north of the southernmost point of the main flow of the lava.

He found a few tracks between the rim of Ceboletta Mesa and the lava beds, and they were fresh tracks. Some went north, some south.

Yet it was only now, seated on the rim of the mesa,

studying the malpais, that he remembered the man who had disappeared from the train the night before his own arrival in Alamitos.

Of course. Kettleman—Flint. And Flint must have left the train during the long climb up the grade, and come westward across the mesa, which meant there was a horse waiting for him.

One of Nugent's riders—Buckdun was a good listener, and he listened to all saloon conversations— had talked of the meeting with the stranger. And it had been west of the railroad. Flint had to be somewhere in this area. Buckdun knew that lava flows had their islands of enclosed grass, their pits and their peaks, their springs and streams. Leaving the train as he had, and dropping from sight so quickly, implied that Flint had proceeded to a destination already known to him.

The story that Jim Flint was actually the kid from The Crossing was too good to keep, and scarcely a person in or around Alamitos but knew of it.

Buckdun was not disturbed. Such a shooting as occurred at The Crossing, and the berserk shooting of Baldwin riders in the saloons of Alamitos following Flint's beating implied a man who lost his head or might become reckless. And the reckless ones are soon the dead ones.

Buckdun, for example, had not a reckless bone in his body. He had refused any previous offer to kill Flint until approached by Lottie Kettleman.

He had never known anyone like her. She was so slender, so dainty, yet so completely a woman. She was breathtakingly lovely, and she knew so well how to talk to a man. She had won him over even before she casually suggested that, as he was going to do it anyway, he might as well go to Baldwin and say he had changed his mind. "After all," she had said, "we...I mean you...can use three thousand dollars."

There had been several of those hints. Buckdun believed he had been promised a great deal when actually he had been promised nothing. He had made no advances for the simple reason that he would not have dared. She was unlike any other woman, something very special, and Flint had made her life miserable.

Buckdun, like many of his kind, was sentimental about things other than his job. The fact that she implied a killing was necessary did not shock him. Lottie had persuaded him...or allowed him to persuade himself, and she had done it without giving anything of herself more than the aura of her presence, her lingering glances, occasional blushes, and the scent of her perfume.

Buckdun was accustomed to dealing with the roughest men, with horses and with guns. His few contacts with women had been on a pay-as-you-leave basis, and Lottie Kettleman was a woman from another world. Like many a lesser man he was conquered by sex. The thought that he should also get the money from Baldwin struck him as eminently practical, and he was amazed that such a pretty little head could think of such a thing.

And now he was here, doing what he did best, stalking a man for the kill.

Flint returned to the hideout and remained there. He slept a lot, drank much beef broth, and cultivated his small garden. He spent a lot of time with his horses, and he broke another of them to ride with no more trouble than had been given him by the red stallion.

Doc McGinnis had told him that rest, freedom from worry, and simple food were the best things for him.

He had always liked reading, and now he had the chance. Usually he took his books to the inner pasture and read, with the horses for company. The weather had grown warmer although the nights were still cool.

On the morning of the fourth day after the shooting in the Divide Saloon he was about to venture out upon the malpais when sunlight winked in his eyes. Turning his head he caught another wink of light from the rim of the mesa. Somebody was up there, probably with field glasses.

He remained absolutely still, knowing that only movement is easily seen, and at such a distance nothing else would reveal his presence.

After several minutes he lowered himself a foot or two then, after a brief wait, dropped back into the basin. It might be that reflected light was not from a field glass, or if so the observer need not be looking for him. But that was not the way to play it. He would assume the worst.

Returning to his seat on the rock he eliminated all from his mind but the problem at hand. If he was being stalked it was because somebody wanted him dead, not an unexpected conclusion in the light of recent events.

The strongest man is he who stands alone. Flint knew he need expect no help from anyone, but then he had never expected help.

From expecting death he had come to want life, and during these past months he had come to a new appreciation of all that was about him, the vast breadth of the western sky, the warmth of the sun, drifting clouds, the gracefulness of a moving horse.

The strong, fine feel of a gun butt in the hand, the smell of leather, the odor of sage on a hot, still day, the twittering of birds, the crunch of sand under the boots, the cold, wonderful feeling of water in the throat after a long thirst, the way a woman moves when she knows an interesting man is watching, the flight of an eagle against the sky, and storm clouds on a summer day...these were things he remembered, he felt, things that he had never appreciated until he thought they would soon be taken from him.

Life, he decided, was never a question of accumulating material things, nor in the struggle for reputation, but in the widening and deepening of perception, increasing the sensitivity of the faculties, of an awareness of the world in which one lives.

Living with this new feeling he had for the first time learned to listen. Disturbed by no people he had become aware of the smallest sound upon the lava beds. The falling of a seed pod, the rustling of a pack rat, the rustle of wind in the grass, the creak of expanding or contracting timbers subjected to heat or cold, all these he knew and his mind separated them from any unfamiliar sound.

Living with awareness had enriched his life, but it had also prepared him for the ordeal that lay before him. His eyes learned to know each natural movement, to place each shadow. If he wished to live he must live with a constant awareness of danger.

They would send Buckdun to kill him.

He must remain near the horses, for their perceptions were quicker than his, and their reactions could be a warning.

He began his arrangements at once. At a point well within the entrance passage he rigged a simple deadfall trap with a large slab of rock balanced to fall. With a thin strap of rawhide about a foot above the ground and well hidden in grass and brush, he prepared his trip and trigger.

Then he sat down in the warm sun and built a bow and an arrow, and this he rigged with the arrow directed down the passage, chest high above the ground. Due to the angle he was able to conceal the bow near one wall. Yet such traps had small chance of success against men like Buckdun, and he might decide to come across the lava itself. Making several trips, after it grew dark, he carried gravel from the stream bed and prepared a wide, apparently accidental belt of it on the sides where the hideout bowl could be approached. Anyone crossing that gravel must make a sound that could be heard below.

He did not for a minute doubt that Buckdun would find him.

From the window of the rock house he could see the bowl itself, the entrance, and part of the rim. After a small meal he lay down on his bunk and, with a carefully hooded light, read until he was sleepy.

At daylight he checked his traps, prepared a lunch, and went into the basin where the horses were kept. Lying on the rim of the lava field above the basin, he studied the terrain with care, knowing such knowledge might mean the difference between life and death. Not far away was one of those ugly pits, all of sixty feet deep, the bottom a litter of knife-edged slabs of rock that had been the roof of the blister. A fall into such a place would mean an ugly death—or eventual starvation.

If it were Buckdun who was stalking him, he would not attempt a shot until reasonably sure of a kill. Flint knew he must appear at odd times or places, establish no system of activity. He settled down to a duel of wits that might last for weeks.

Surprisingly, he found himself filled with zest for the coming trial. Where would Buckdun make his first try? Where would the hunter seek the hunted?

At the creek. Every man needed water, so Buckdun would expect Flint to come to the stream. And that was the one thing he must not do. He would get his water from within the cave, for Buckdun must be led into aggression and not allowed simply to wait. A man who moves is a man who risks, and Buckdun must be forced to stalk.

So began the strange duel that was to end in the death of one man, perhaps of two.

On the third morning after the fight in the Divide Saloon that broke Baldwin's strength in Alamitos, the Kaybar hands had established camp on the old headquarters site, and cleared the charred timbers to rebuild. Ed Flynn, now able to sit up, was directing the construction of temporary quarters.

Short of sundown Buckdun rode into camp.

Nancy Kerrigan stood by the fire where Juana was cooking, and Rockley squatted on his heels drinking coffee. Gaddis had just carried coffee to Flynn, and he stopped beside him and turned to face Buckdun.

"Got you a start," Buckdun indicated the cleared area. "How's chances for coffee?"

" 'Light and set.' " Nancy used the customary term, but her tone indicated no welcome. "No man was ever turned from Kaybar without a meal."

"Riding through," Buckdun explained, accepting a cup from Juana. Nothing in the camp escaped his eyes, but Nancy was sure it was nothing in camp that brought him here.

"When you have had your coffee," Nancy said, "you can ride on. I don't want you on Kaybar range."

He lifted his cold, bleak eyes to hers. "I have troubled none of your people."

"And you won't. If you are on Kaybar range after daybreak tomorrow you'll be shot on sight. Any rider of mine who sees you and doesn't open fire upon you, or any rider who offers you an even break, will be fired."

"That's hard talk." Buckdun refilled his cup from the pot and looked at her with grudging admiration. "I'll be careful, ma'am, but believe me, I'm not after your people."

"Did you tell Tom Nugent that?"

His expression did not change. "I never talked to Tom Nugent. I know nothing about him."

Rockley stood up. "Finish your coffee," he said, "and get out."

Buckdun looked at him mildly. "You may come to town some day."

"I'll be there often," Rockley replied, "and if you want it that way we can extend Kaybar range to cover Alamitos and hunt you there."

"If any rider of mine is shot," Nancy added, "we

will hunt you down and hang you where we find you. Is that clear?"

"Nothing could be plainer," Buckdun said. He crossed to his horse and stepped into the saddle. He looked down at her, standing straight and lovely beside the campfire. "Ma'am, folks have said disparaging things about lady bosses. I reckon they were wrong. You'll do to ride the river with."

"I doubt if he'll give us trouble," Nancy said when he had ridden away. "But my orders stand."

"He's not just riding," Rockley said, "he's hunting."

A faint dust hung in the air upon the trail where he had gone, and Nancy felt a little shiver.

"He'll get what he goes after," Milt Ryan said.

"He'll kill Flint," Scott said. "You know it's him he's after."

And after that nobody spoke while the shadows gathered and the bats began to appear, circling upon their ceaseless quest for insects in the night air.

Where was he now? Where was Flint?

Nancy walked from the fire and Johnny Otero, with worry in his eyes, watched her go. She paused and looked where the ridges were a dark line against the deep blue where the stars were.

Flint was out there somewhere—alone.

CHAPTER 18

IT WAS VERY hot. The far horizon was piled high with gigantic masses of cumulus, but under the brassy sky the lava was burning to the touch. Buckdun lay in the shade of a stunted pine that grew from a crack in the rock, and watched the stream.

Two days ago he had been confident this would prove a trap for Flint but now he was no longer sure. Obviously there was some other source from which he could obtain water.

Nothing moved but a buzzard against the sun-filled sky. Flint was down there, he was sure. Two days before he found part of a track made by a freshly shod horse in wind-drifted sand near the lava. A few hours later he found the crack that provided access to the hideout, but he was wary of tight places. However, there were tracks within the crack, a number of them.

He must see more of the bowl. Taking his rifle he moved out of the shade. He wore hard-soled Apache-style moccasins and carried an extra pair in his haversack. He also carried jerked meat and a little tea. If necessary he could live for a week on what was in that pack.

Making no more noise than a prowling coyote, Buckdun moved across the lava, his eyes on the rim of the bowl. Eager for a glimpse of the interior, he stepped into the edge of the gravel, and his moccasin grated ever so slightly.

Instantly he was still. He knew the belt of gravel for what it was and swore softly. Lowering himself to a crouch, he remained where he was, listening.

He straightened up finally and took a long step forward to try and clear the gravel. A bullet whipped by his skull. He hit the rock and rolled over and over to get into a crack. He wound up, rifle ready, but panting and genuinely scared.

He waited and listened, but the blue sky drifted with puffballs of cloud and there was no sound beneath it. But that angry, whiplike sound of the bullet and the racketing report remained with him. It was the first time in six years, aside from the ineffectual shots fired by Ed Flynn, that he had been shot at, and he had not even seen where the shot came from.

He waited the afternoon through, knowing Flint would have seen where he went to the ground, and unable to shift his position from lack of nearby cover. Only when darkness came did he move. A tuft of brush had been placed on the pommel of his saddle, and adorning one sprig was an empty cartridge shell.

That shell was a mute reminder that Flint, had he wished, might have been lying in wait, and Buckdun led his horse some distance before mounting. Two hours later, after lunch and tea, he returned for another attempt.

Despite himself, he was worried. Was he losing his grip? Before, he had done the stalking, but now he himself was stalked.

He entered the crack and, after listening, slowly

began to move ahead. If he could get into the basin and be waiting when Flint came out in the morning...

He had a cramped, closed-in feeling and an urge to get out. He rounded a corner and took a step forward. Something tugged at his ankle and instinctively he threw himself back and to the side.

In one wild instant he knew he had blundered into a trap. He heard rock grate upon rock. There was a tremendous crash, then dust stifled him, and he lay with his palms flat on the ground, gasping for breath. It took several minutes before the pounding of his heart slowed down and he realized he was unhurt. Panic surged through him. Get out...and get out fast!

Grabbing up his rifle he fled down the passage for a dozen yards before stopping. Panting, he listened for any sound of pursuit, and heard nothing, only a faint trickle of falling sand.

He considered the situation. Why not go back now? Another trap was possible but unlikely. Turning, he started back, climbing over the fallen rock. His hand touched the rock wall and it was cold...cold. He felt a momentary dread. Was it a premonition? Angrily, he shook off the feeling. This was just a job like any other. He took a step forward and, distrusting the rustling grass, moved to the side of the crevice.

It was a sudden move and it saved his life, for as he turned he tripped the trigger on the second trap. The arrow intended for his chest ripped his sleeve and dug deep into the muscle on the end of his shoulder.

He dropped to his knees, ready for a quick shot, sure it had been a direct attack rather than a trap, but after a minute or two there was no sound and his shoulder began to hurt. He put his hand up and it came away wet. He swore bitterly under his breath and got out his bandanna to stop the bleeding. Then he took up his rifle and went into the bowl, concealing himself in some brush.

Overhead the sky was but little lighter than the darkness within the bowl. Somewhere a small animal dislodged a rock and it fell softly into the grass. Water whispered over the stones. Buckdun eased his back against the rock and bit off a hunk of jerky. Methodically, he began to chew.

This could be a death trap. Suppose while he waited for Flint that Flint waited for *him*?

When daylight came Buckdun saw a patch of cropped grass, a patch of garden, and a walled-in overhang with no visible entrance. There was no horse, no sign of life. He waited an hour, then another. Sunlight was bright above the rock house but the crack that gave entrance to the bowl was in shadow. With growing impatience, Buckdun waited.

FLINT HAD SPENT the night in the inner basin close to the horses, and had slept soundly, knowing they would warn him of the approach of any man or animal.

He prepared coffee and a small breakfast, meanwhile scanning the basin pasture with care. When he had eaten he went to the cave and passed through the tunnel. Opening the manger-concealed door, he stepped into the house.

From well back inside he studied the entrance

through his field glass. The trap was sprung. The area was only a few square yards but with the glass he could examine it thoroughly and, knowing every inch, he could see it had been entered.

A bee found its way in and droned about the room. In a cottonwood tree a mockingbird ran through his repertoire.

When an hour had passed he decided whoever was there would not make the first move. He went back through the manger and leaned a slab of rock against the inside of the door.

The idea came to him suddenly and he was amused by it. Slipping out of the inner basin, he crossed the lava. Coming down off the malpais, it took him only a few minutes to find Buckdun's horse. Mounting, he started up the trail for Alamitos.

It was midafternoon when he reached Alamitos and, tying Buckdun's horse at the rail, he went into the Divide Saloon. Baldwin was at the bar with two strangers, obviously eastern men. Baldwin glanced at Flint, and then at Buckdun's horse.

"That's right, it *is* Buckdun's horse. He's out in the hills hunting me."

"He'll find you, too."

"Isn't that what you hired him for? To kill me?"

Porter Baldwin fought back his anger. "I don't know what you're talking about," he replied, and his face turned a deep red.

Flint ordered a drink. "Who else has the money to hire Buckdun? Who does he see when he goes in the back door of the hotel?"

The two strangers looked uneasy, and glanced at Baldwin. Flint tossed off his drink and went out, walking to the hotel dining room. He was eating the best meal they offered when the door opened and Lottie Kettleman came in.

She looked at him suspiciously. "Jim, what are you doing here?"

"As you see, I am enjoying a good meal...Lottie, you're not looking well. I don't believe this climate agrees with you."

"I don't know what you're feeling so good about," she said irritably. "Nothing has changed."

"Do you know Buckdun, Lottie?"

Her face was without expression. "Who? I don't place the name."

"You'd better go back to New York, Lottie. I want no more trouble with you."

"What are you talking about?"

"Only two people could afford to pay Buckdun. You or Baldwin, and I am quite sure you would not spend that kind of money if you could get someone to do it for you."

"Are you trying to frighten me?"

"You are like your father, Lottie. This scheme is like one of his—all scheme and no achievement. Why don't you marry some nice guy and make an end to all this?"

"I am married—to you."

"If I return I shall file suit for divorce, and if you contest it I will present the Pinkerton file as evidence. They may not hang you, but they will send you to prison. I want my freedom."

"So you can marry that ranch girl?"

"Merely to be free."

She was very pale and her eyes were bright and hard. "Suppose you don't come back?"

"Why, then, I shall leave you to Buckdun. You'd try to cheat him, and I know what will happen then." He refilled his cup. "Get on the train, Lottie, and go away from here as fast as you can."

The moon was over the mountains when he climbed back on the lava, but he saw nothing and heard nothing, and his horses were feeding quietly. Buckdun was still around, and when he found his horse with its saddle hidden, he would know it had been used.

Flint had ridden to Alamitos not on a whim, but deliberately, hoping to anger Buckdun into carelessness. Under no illusions about the man he faced, Flint knew he had been lucky to escape alive thus far.

Shifting to a corner of the lava wall away from his bed, Flint sat down and, leaning back against the wall, he slept.

Dawn was in the sky when he awakened, but the horizon was dark with thunderheads, laced with patterns of lightning. A dampness in the air warned of the coming storm.

For thirty minutes, Flint studied every cranny within reach of his eyes, and when he moved it was against the wall, utilizing every bit of brush for concealment.

At his camp he stuffed his slicker pockets with food, and the pockets of his pants and coat with cartridges. Then he risked a small fire under the overhang. After he had his coffee he doused the fire and took up his rifle.

As he moved away from the camp he was trusting

the horses and almost missed the warning. He looked around in time to see the red stallion's head come up sharply, and he dropped to his hands, hearing the whip-crack of a bullet as he did so.

The horses had run off a short distance but were looking past him, so turning about he crawled and slid along the grass with his rifle across his arms in front of him. Reaching the front of the ice cave, where the ground fell away sharply, he took shelter and peered through a small space between the rocks. He was shifting his head to peer through at a different angle when a bullet struck the rock within inches of his face, then ricocheted into the depths of the cave.

He crouched, hesitating. Would Buckdun expect him to move to right or left? One thing Buckdun would not expect would be a shot from the place where the bullet struck.

Risking a glance, Flint decided the only place Buckdun could use for shelter was a hummock of lava on the rim about sixty yards away. From his study of the terrain he recalled that the hummock was not thick, and most lava was quite porous in that area. Lifting the rifle, he drove three fast shots at the hummock of rock, then moved off twenty yards in a crouching run and took another shot. His standing for that shot was perfectly synchronized with a movement by Buckdun, but Flint fired too quickly and the bullet missed.

For an hour, nothing happened.

Then he heard a stone strike rock. From the force of the impact he knew it was thrown. After a brief wait he worked his way back to the ice cave, remembering that a few days before he had seen a crack or blowhole that allowed a little light to fall into the cave. He had not investigated to see if the hole was large enough to permit him to get through, but now he did so. It was a vent made by escaping gases long ago. He climbed through, and scrambled out into a clump of rock slabs and brush, tearing his hand cruelly on the rough lava.

Momentarily blinded by a flash of lightning that struck somewhere near, he lay still, awaiting the crash of thunder. It came, and with it, the rain.

It came with a roar and a rush. Lightning crashed and the smell of brimstone was in his nostrils and thunder rolled and reverberated against the walls of the mesa. The rain swept across the malpais in driving sheets and then, through the downpour, he saw Buckdun.

Dimly visible, Buckdun was running across the lava five hundred yards away. Snapping his rifle to his shoulder, Flint squeezed off three shots, saw Buckdun veer sharply to break his line of fire, then vanish into some crack or hollow.

There was no shelter atop the lava, but Flint was determined to waste no time. Rising, he moved as swiftly as possble over the lava to get around the end of the basin. Once he heard a dull boom under his feet and felt an instant of fear, but his next step took him to solid rock.

Avoiding smooth patches that might conceal death pits beneath them, he scrambled over rough and broken lava, slipping once and skinning his knees. When he was around the end of the basin, he slowed down. His slicker was close to the color of the basaltic rock, and he moved now with great care.

A shot came from nowhere and something struck his shin a wicked blow. His leg buckled and he went down. But when he pulled up his pant leg he saw only a great, rapidly growing swelling, split along the top. He had been struck by a fragment of rock knocked loose by the bullet.

He hunched behind a hummock of lava until the numbness went out of his leg, but when he started to move, it was with a limp. He had a badly bruised shinbone, nearly as painful if not as incapacitating as a break.

There would be no letup now. He was in a fight to the death, and with an opponent superior to him in bushwhacking skill, and he must never remain for long in one place. Whatever else he was, Buckdun was a master hand at his business.

Flint moved now, half running, half crawling, utilizing every bit of cover. Once a shot clipped a bush near his head, another time a bullet burned the back of his calf as he jerked it from sight.

He saw nothing at which to shoot. Apparently Buckdun was working with some scheme in mind. Suddenly, Flint looked around, and his quick glance took the wind out of him. For an instant he felt as if he had been hit in the belly by a stiff punch. Behind him was a wall of rock all of thirty feet high. Here the lava had come up, poured over and flowed away, leaving the cliff a sheer face that blocked all passage.

He had been cleverly herded like a sheep into a cul-de-sac from which there seemed no escape. To go back the way he had come he must first advance, going directly toward Buckdun's gun. And that was exactly what Buckdun would expect him to do.

He was under cover. For the moment he was invisible to the hunter, and he glanced quickly around. There was a dip in the rock, a gully worn by water pouring down over the lava toward the depression at the foot of the wall. Ducking into it, he ran bent over, straight to the wall.

To the right there was a blank wall, then one of those pits. He went that way, but there was a sheer drop, the edge running back under his feet. In the bottom was the jagged rock that had once been the roof of the pit. Among the rocks grew a few pines, some of them seventy feet, but their tops still below the rim.

Turning, he went back in the opposite direction. He had but a few minutes, and there was no cover here, nor any concealment.

He paused, knowing that a little thought was better than a lot of running. He could wait, but he could be butchered from cover if he waited, without ever seeing a target for return fire.

He went on to the left, and there the wall took a sharp bend, falling back several feet before continuing on. Nowhere was there a break, nor was there any cover.

And then he saw his chance.

Here, where the rock wall jogged, there was a chimney. It was a crack in the wall that widened toward the top. Here at the bottom it was about level with his head, but only a few inches wide. Toward the top it became at least four feet wide.

Yet, if he was in that crack when Buckdun came upon him, he would have no chance. He would be caught there, trapped like a rabbit in a snare, to be shot at will.

And he did not even know if he could get into the crack and reach the top. He might fall. He had heard of rock climbers doing such things, but had never attempted it himself. But it was his only chance, and he was going to try.

The corner of the wall was out of sight of Buckdun until he came far toward this side, and he would have to hope that Buckdun did not make it until he had reached the top . . . if he could do it at all.

He looked up at the V-shaped crack. There was no place to get a proper handhold. The sharp V left no room for the fingers of even one hand.

Somewhere behind him a foot scraped on stone. He took one quick glance up, slung his rifle, and jumped upward.

CHAPTER 19

WITH HIS LEFT fist lifted high, Flint jumped and thrust the closed fist into the crack. The fist jammed there and he muscled himself up until he could get a hold on the side of the crack with his right hand. Releasing his fist, he took an opposite hold with it and worked his way higher until he could get a foot in the crack.

When the crack was wide enough he put his back against one side, his knee against the other, and worked his way up until he could get both knees against the side of the rock chimney. He struggled upward, opposing his back to his knees until he could grasp the edge with his left hand.

Below he heard the rattle of rocks, displaced by his exertions, and then the scrape of a moccasin or boot.

Gasping for breath, he kept himself braced. He must swing his right arm, grasp the edge, then pull himself over. If Buckdun showed while he was hanging there, he would be killed.

He had no time to waste. He swung his right arm across and up, and at the same time relaxed his pressure against the two sides of the crack. For an instant he hung there; then, with a tremendous heave, he pulled himself up and swung his leg over the rim.

He caught a glimpse of a dark figure below, felt the rain beating on his face, then rolled up and away, even as a bullet nicked the rim where he had been a moment before.

He lay flat on the wet rock, his lungs pumping at the air. Then slowly he pushed back a little farther and took the rifle from its sling. Only then did he look around.

The terrain here was like that below: higher, and with a wide view of broken lava and pock-marking pits. He got up and looked off in the distance. The hideout was not visible from here. He could see green where the basin pasture was, and far off to the south and west, an even larger area of green, enclosed by lava, undoubtedly the Hole-in-the-Wall.

He walked away from the rim, stepping carefully because of the knife-edged corrugations of the lava flow.

Buckdun crouched in the partial shelter of an overhang and cursed the driving rain. It destroyed visibility, made hunting a hazard. And it was a cold rain.

He made a small fire, considered what had happened so far, and felt a mounting depression. Nothing had been going right. With grudging admiration he reflected that he had never been sent after a man like this before. Who would think that a man could scale that cliff without wings? Yet Flint had done it.

He made himself a cup of tea. Flint was not going anywhere. Ordinarily Buckdun would have been afraid the man he hunted would get clean away, but Flint meant to see it through. Chewing on a piece of jerky, Buckdun sipped his tea, and stared gloomily at the gray, rain-screened world.

His shoulder was stiff and sore from the arrow wound, his pants were torn, and he was wet. There were a dozen cuts and abrasions on his hide from contact with the lava. Lightning flashed in the distance and he listened to the thunder roll its drums up a canyon, somewhere. He sipped his tea. Time to be getting on with it. He had a man to kill.

The bullet smashed the cup from his fingers and smacked viciously into the stunted pine under which he was sitting.

Buckdun rolled back quickly, his finger stinging from the violence that had smashed the cup from his hand. He reached out and grasped his rifle, snaking it to him. The bullet had surprised and shocked him deeply . . . he had been sure Flint would either remain atop the cliff or would take much more time in getting around it.

He started to rise, and three more bullets beat a rapid tattoo of searching fire. The first smashed into his small fire, scattering the sticks and sprinkling his sleeve with embers, the second drilled into the solid blackness of the tree, which might at a distance have seemed to be his body, and the third cut across his knuckles.

He crawled into the brush, and looked up to see Flint bearing down upon him. He whipped up his rifle and, springing free of the tangle, shot from the hip while he was still moving. Flint disappeared. Buckdun slipped into a deep crack in the lava, hung by his fingers, then let go and dropped to the bottom. He ran in the direction from which the shots had come, emerging in a rock-choked basin with high walls. Another bullet smashed near him; he squeezed between two rocks, gasping for breath and sobbing with fury.

He stopped to reload, although there were still

shells in the chamber. That Flint—there was a wicked bite to those shots he was firing, and his rifle obviously packed tremendous power.

Buckdun looked at the back of his hand and there was a streak of bloody flesh across three knuckles.

I'm getting out of here, he told himself suddenly. To hell with it, and to hell with them.

Buckdun dropped to his hands and knees and crawled into the blackness of a cave in the basin wall. There was a shard of ancient pottery there, and an arrowhead of a kind he had never seen. He knelt with his rifle and waited. The rain fell unceasingly, although without its earlier violence. The thunder sulked in the distance, and the sky was low and gray, clouds swollen with rain. It could not be long until dark.

He had no idea where he was.

FLINT WAS EXHAUSTED. He moved into the area from which he had driven Buckdun, and picked up the battered cup. The haversack which Buckdun had carried was there, and he found the small cache of tea and made a cup for himself. It had been sheer luck that he found a way down from the cliff, and happened to see the faint blue of smoke against the clouds and rain.

Yet he dared not stay here. He gulped the tea, then dropped the cup and moved away. He limped badly, for his shin was black and hugely swollen where the rock had struck it. His palms were torn from scrambling in the lava, and his knees skinned. His muscles were heavy with weariness and he had no idea how much country he had covered.

The rain still fell, and he felt as if he carried the burden of the storm on his sagging shoulders. The rifle was heavy and he had lost one of his pistols—somewhere back in the basin pasture, he thought.

Flint wanted shelter and he wanted rest. He took a sight on the cliff from which he had first descended and started back, working his way with less caution than the situation demanded. He knew he had driven Buckdun to ground somewhere in the rock, but he was not up to standing by, keeping alert for any move.

He dearly wanted rest.

It was two miles to the basin pasture and he made it there, falling only once. He ripped his pant leg again and tore the flesh of his knee wickedly, ripping it deep this time.

He climbed back down into the basin. The horses were huddled at the ice cave, and he avoided them. He would get back into the hideout and have a fire. He would be warm once more, even if it was the last time. He scarcely could remember a time when he had not been cold and wet.

All through the bitter, long day they had run, climbed, and exchanged shots. He had come close... perhaps Buckdun was wounded.

He got back to the rock house and built a roaring fire. He pulled off his clothing and rubbed himself dry with a blanket. Then he dressed again, in dry clothes, still shivering with cold. He made coffee, and put the beans on to warm up, dumping the can into the pot and then, after a thoughtful look, another can.

He seated himself on the bunk and wiped his rifle dry, running a patch through the barrel. Then he dried the Smith & Wesson and checked the loads. He unloaded and reloaded the rifle after wiping the ammunition for fear some dirt had gotten on it during the wild flight of the day.

He barred the door. The window was too small for anything larger than a cat, and the entrance through the manger next to impossible to find, but he blocked that door also.

When at last he fell upon the bunk and pulled the blankets around him he was still shaking with cold, and he was exhausted.

NANCY KERRIGAN WAS in Alamitos when Buckdun rode into town. Along the street people stopped and stared or peered from windows. The big gunman was dog-weary and soaked to the hide. One hand was wrapped in a rough bandage and his face was drawn and haggard.

He drew up at the general store and half-fell from the saddle. He stopped on the walk, under the awning on which the rain drummed, and looked up and down the street, then went inside. He bought two boxes of shells, then said, "Got any dynamite?"

He bought fifty sticks, and the caps and fuses to go with them. Wrapped in an extra slicker to keep it dry, and with a new slicker for himself he was ready to go back. Instead he went to the livery barn, put up his horse and returned to the Grand Hotel. Within minutes he was stretched out and sound asleep.

Nancy Kerrigan went to the store. "Howard, what did that man buy?"

"Shells. He bought shells and he bought some dynamite, ma'am," Howard said. "I'd say he had something holed up he wanted to blast out."

Nancy left quickly and went to the Divide Saloon. At the door she paused. No one was there whom she could send inside. Gathering her skirts, she pushed open the door.

"Red," she called, "is Milt Ryan in there? Or any of my outfit?"

There was the scrape of a chair, and Ryan showed up in the door. "Howdy, ma'am. Something wrong?" Rockley and Gaddis were behind him.

"Milt, could you backtrack Buckdun? He's gone to the hotel, and from his looks I'd say he was dog-tired and ready for bed. I want to backtrack him. He's got Jim Flint holed up somewhere and he's bought dynamite."

"Dynamite? Well, now."

Ryan squinted at the street and at the rain coming down. "Reckon I could, ma'am. If the rain down thataway hasn't washed his tracks plumb out."

"Pete," Nancy said, "get your horses. Get mine, too. We're going to find him. I'll have no man blasted with dynamite. At least"—she looked at Pete and smiled—"not a man that good."

Pete Gaddis hesitated. He glanced at Rockley and at Milt Ryan. "There's an easier way, ma'am," Pete said. "We can go get Buckdun."

"No. You'd get him but one of you might be killed. No, we'll find Flint and take him to the Kaybar."

Nancy Kerrigan had made one stop—at the general store—and bought a rifle. Her own was back at the ranch. Then they started south, holding to a space-eating trot.

The men exchanged looks and Milt Ryan's icy eyes showed a touch of amusement and of genuine pleasure.

There was no trouble with the trail, for the Buckdun horse had been stepping out and its hooves had taken a deep bite. Nor had anyone else been along since the rain. When the tracks ended they could see where the horse had stood for some time.

"I'd say that there horse was here most of the day," Milt said.

"There were shots earlier," Rockley said. "When I went back in the Hole after the horses I could hear shooting, off in the lava somewhere."

Buckdun had seen no necessity to conceal his trail. The tracks led to the lava beds and right to the crack in the rock.

"We're facing up to trouble, ma'am," Rockley advised. "That Buckdun, he'll come back down here. I figure he won't sleep more than a couple of hours at most, because he figures he's got his man where he wants him. He won't take kindly to us messing around with his affairs."

"We will brand that steer when we get to it," Nancy replied. "Let's get inside."

They started along the crack, but coming to the fallen boulder, they halted, made doubtful by its presence. Then they went on, and entered the small basin.

There was the garden, its neat rows of crops weeded and tended, but there was no sign of a horse, and at first they did not see the walled-up overhang where the house was. Milt Ryan worked his way over there and they gathered around.

"A body would be a fool to go to pounding on that door," Rockley commented, "with an upset man in there expecting trouble. Most likely he will shoot right through it."

Nancy did not reply. She walked up and, standing to the side of the door, she reached over and rapped loudly. "Jim! Jim Flint!"

After several minutes she heard muffled sounds, and then Jim said, "Who is it?"

"It's Nancy, Jim. Nancy Kerrigan. I've three of the boys with me. Buckdun's in town buying dynamite."

The door opened, and the first thing Nancy saw was the pant leg soaked with blood. The leg below was swollen, the material stretched tight.

"You've been hurt," she said. "Let me see what I can do."

"No," he said. "If Buckdun's bringing dynamite, you'd better get out. He'll probably drop it down from above."

"He'll do that," Ryan said, "and if we all take out we'll be better off."

"Go ahead," Flint said, "I'm staying." As Nancy started to interrupt, he added, "I've got to. If a man starts running there's no place to stop."

She looked at him, her eyes clinging to his. "Jim . . . Jim, you'll be hurt."

"When this is over, I'm planning to ride around to see you. Will you be home, Nancy?"

"You do that, Jim. I'll be home. You just come around, and you plan on staying awhile. We're building again, and there will be a place for you."

"Pete," Flint said, "get her away from here. If I know Buckdun he's on his way back now."

When they had gone he went in the house. Others knew of it now. This place where he had come to die, so long a secret, was secret no more.

He stuffed shells in his pocket and picked up his rifle and his slicker. The sky was overcast and there were rumblings of thunder. He walked outside and looked around, then went back in and through the manger.

The horses came eagerly but he spoke to them. Then Flint climbed up on the lava, and started to work his way back toward the hideout.

Night was coming, and thunder was rumbling. A spatter of rain started, threw a quick flurry of drops, and then raced over the lava beds and away. In flashes of lightning he could see the fringe of dark trees along the mesa's edge.

Ahead of him was a wide, somewhat swelling expanse of open rock, part of it covering the tunnel that led from the hideout to the basin pasture. When he first saw the head he thought it was a rock. It was still for a long time but finally, looking past it so as not to blur his vision, Flint saw the object move and rise. And a man stood there, just beyond the swell, and he had a package in his arm.

The man started forward, carrying the package in one hand and his rifle in the other, going toward the rim of the lava flow. Jim Flint lifted his rifle and Buckdun was dead in his sights, but he could not fire.

Flint stood up, his rifle in his right hand. "Buckdun!" he said, and thunder rolled like far-off drums.

Buckdun turned and looked at him. There was no

more than forty yards between them, and Buckdun's tall figure stood stark against the gray sky.

"So this is the way it is going to be, is it?" Buckdun asked. "Well, you've given me a fair chase."

He spoke casually, but his rifle moved fast. Jim Flint tipped up the muzzle of his own rifle, caught the barrel with his left hand and shot from the hip. Buckdun's shot was a split second too late. He staggered, dropped his rifle, and fell to one knee.

Flint held his fire, but stood with his legs spread, rifle ready for a shot. "Well, you got me then," Buckdun said. "I'd like a smoke . . . is it all right?"

"Have your smoke."

Buckdun's face gleamed momentarily in the glare of the match, the light showing the hard planes, then he bent his head, shielding the flare of the match with his body. When he turned the cigarette was between his lips.

He stood up and a spark dropped away behind him. "You have given me a rough time of it, Flint. Tell me, is it true you were the kid at The Crossing?"

Something in his tone was wrong, some sound, some faint suggestion of . . . another spark dropped away behind him, and another.

Flint felt a shock of panic. "Damn you! Buckdun—!"

The killer's hand swung around in an arc, in it a black bulking bundle from which sparks were shooting.

The *dynamite!*

Flint fired, working the action as fast as he could move his hands. He saw Buckdun jerk with the impact of the heavy rifle at close range, saw the black bundle slip from his hand to the rock before him, saw him fall sprawling as the second bullet hit him, then leap to grab up the bundle of dynamite again. Buckdun sprang forward for an easier throw but there was a sharp crack of splintering rock and he vanished from sight.

Flint threw himself to the rock and as he did so there was a thunderous roar and a tremendous blast of flame, and then rocks were raining about him, and he lay still until the last few had fallen, and then he got shakily to his feet.

He walked forward, tapping the rock under foot with his rifle to make sure it was solid. When lightning flashed, he could see a pit littered with broken rock, and the sprawled body of Buckdun.

He heard them coming before they reached him. "Jim! Jim! Jim, is it you?"

"I'm all right, Nancy," he said, "I'm all right."

CHAPTER 20

AFTER THE RAIN the air was washed clean. The unpainted buildings of Alamitos still showed dampness, but the dust had been washed from the brick buildings and the adobes seemed freshened after the storm. The cottonwood leaves rustled pleasurably, and the few horses at the hitching rail were quick to lift their heads when the Kaybar rode into town.

As if by prearrangement they scattered themselves along the street and Nancy went at once to the Grand Hotel, escorted by Jim Flint.

He wore a gray suit this morning, but the wide hat of a western man. On the steps they paused.

"You're sure you have to do this?"

"I have to do it."

"All right." She looked him straight in the eye. "My father always told me there were things a man had to do. Just see that you do it well."

He smiled suddenly, and she was amazed at how his face lit up. "Why, I'll do that," he said, "I surely will!"

Porter Baldwin had been standing in front of the Divide Saloon and Jim Flint turned and walked down the street toward him. The big man stood awaiting him, his huge body bulking heavy in his black broadcloth suit.

"He's dead, Port."

Baldwin took the cigar from his mouth and looked at it with displeasure. He tossed it into the street. "Who's dead?"

"Buckdun. He caught it last night down in the lava beds."

Baldwin stared at him. "So? What's that to me?"

"I just thought you'd like to know, Port. Now you are going to go down to the station and get on that train and leave town—and you're never coming back."

"Is that right?"

"It is. You can go willingly, or you can be loaded on like a side of beef. The choice is yours."

"Noticed you favoring your leg. Something wrong?"

"There isn't much time, Port."

"I suppose if I don't go," Baldwin said, "you'll use a gun on me?"

"Why, no, Port. From what I hear fists are your weapons. Knuckle and skull and no holds barred... am I right?"

"You'd not be fool enough to tackle me that way," Port replied. He lifted his hands. "I've killed a man with these."

"It's a trouble I have, Port. I am a fool." And Flint hit him.

The punch was quick, a darting left jab that slid between Baldwin's half-lifted hands and hit him in the mouth.

Baldwin lifted a hand to his smashed lips and looked at the blood on his fingers. "I think I'll take off my coat," he said, "because to judge by that punch it will take me more than a minute."

They removed their coats very calmly, then their ties and collars; they faced each other and Baldwin doubled his huge fists and took his stance. "Now, Jim Kettleman, I am going to kill you with my hands."

"Put your money where your mouth is," Flint replied. "I'll bet you five thousand dollars I can whip you."

"Now, I like a sporting man. I'll cover that. And we have witnesses to the fact."

A considerable crowd had gathered, and the two men circled warily within the circle they created. Flint was under no false impression of what lay before him. His leg was stiff and sore and he was not in the best of shape after the long struggle on the malpais.

Moreover, understanding the man he faced, he knew that only a beating with fists would mean defeat for Baldwin. Only that would send him back to New York. Alamitos had troubles enough without coping with Baldwin's devious conniving, and the fact that he was still here was evidence enough that whatever he intended to do was not yet complete.

Flint circled briefly, then feinted a left to the body, and when Baldwin dropped a hand to block the punch, Flint hit him in the mouth, the feint and the punch one smooth, continued action. The punch jolted against Baldwin's teeth.

"I'm getting tired of that," Baldwin said, and he came in fast. Flint's stiff leg slowed him, and he caught a wicked right to the side of the face that rocked him to his heels. He was driven back by the weight of Baldwin's charging body, and the bigger man's hammering fists landed to the head and body. Ducking his head against Baldwin's shoulder, Flint caught the other man's right wrist under his arm and, clasping Baldwin's right elbow in his left hand, he spun the big man off balance and hit him in the belly.

Releasing him suddenly, Flint followed up with two hard blows to the head before Baldwin could get set. Then toe to toe they stood and slugged.

Baldwin's wind was surprisingly good, and he knew what he was doing. He bulled Flint back into the hitch rail which splintered beneath him and they both fell to the ground. Baldwin smashed a right at Flint's head, but Flint rolled out of the way and caught Baldwin's sleeve at the shoulder and jerked. Coupled with the weight behind the punch, the jerk took Baldwin off balance. Flint bucked him off and scrambled to his feet.

Baldwin lunged at him from a runner's starting position, driving Flint back and into the dust. Rushing in, Baldwin swung a kick at Flint's head, but Flint threw his weight against Baldwin's anchoring leg.

They fought bitterly, brutally, driving, punching, butting, without letup. Flint's breath was coming in ragged gasps. For the first time, under the bigger man's weight and the driving pace, he was realizing how much his illness had taken out of him. He was in no shape for a long fight.

He had to slow the bigger man down, and Baldwin handled himself well. Flint feinted a left and smashed Baldwin under the heart with a hard right. He took two stiff punches but belted Baldwin in the stomach again. Boxing more carefully, he landed two long lefts to the body.

Baldwin backed away and ripped the last shreds of his shirt from his body, flexing his big hands. Shrewdly, he could see that Flint favored one leg, and that his condition was not too good. Bobbing his head to duck Flint's left, he crowded close and knocked Flint to the ground.

Deliberately Baldwin fell, dropping his knee to strike Flint's injured leg. Flint grunted, feeling pain knife through him, sure the leg was bleeding again, for it was cut deeply in one place, horribly bruised in another. Baldwin swung both fists to Flint's head, and then rested his left hand on Flint's chest and drew back his right for a final blow.

Flint struck swiftly at the left hand. Baldwin lost balance as his hand was knocked away. Flint rolled free and got up. He was bloody and battered, his breath coming in gasps, one eye monstrously swollen from a blow.

Baldwin struck him with a left, then measured him with another. Flint caught his sleeve, stepped in quickly, and threw Baldwin over his back with a flying mare. Baldwin hit the ground hard and Flint backed away.

His leg was stiffening, and there was a searing pain in his side. But he had his second wind and suddenly he felt good.

Baldwin got up. "I think you're through," he said, walking toward Flint, and Flint knew he looked it. Despite the sudden feeling that came with his second wind there was the knowledge that there could not be much left within him in the way of strength. He must win now.

Baldwin, too, had been hurt. But now he stepped

in and swung, incredibly fast. Flint stepped in swiftly, slipping the punch, and smashed a right to the heart. It was a perfectly timed, perfectly executed punch, and Baldwin's mouth dropped open in time to catch a sweeping left hook.

Baldwin's knees buckled and he fell face forward, into the dust.

"Why, now," Flint said, "I think that does it."

Turning, he went to the water trough and started to bathe away the blood.

A scream brought him sharply around. Baldwin was coming at him with a three-foot length of the broken hitch rail and, as Flint turned, Baldwin swung viciously. Flint dove under the swing and knocked Baldwin back against the wall of the building with such force he heard cans fall from the shelves inside. Then Flint balled his fist and hit Baldwin. He hit him once, then again.

Picking Baldwin up bodily, he threw him, like a sack of grain, against the trough. He picked him up once more and shoved him back against the wall. "I don't want to hit you again," Flint said, "but you owe me five thousand dollars."

Porter Baldwin stared at Flint, and it was in him to try again, but he had been fairly whipped and knew it. Moreover, Buckdun was dead and the game was played out.

"You must take my check," he said, through swollen lips. "I've not that much in cash."

"With your fists you're an honest man, and I'll take your check. You'll be wanting to write it before train time."

They went in the store and, while Baldwin fumbled

with a pen in his swollen fist, Flint threw a dollar on the counter, took down a fresh shirt and put it on.

"There you are," Baldwin pushed the check toward him. "It was surely won. I didn't think the man lived who could tear down my meathouse."

Lottie Kettleman was in the dining room when they walked in, and she said, "So you have beaten him, then? I knew you would."

Jim reached into his pocket and took out a small jeweled medallion. "This is yours, Lottie. I found it in Buckdun's pocket. I will be writing to Burroughs and he will arrange a divorce."

"You're staying here, then?"

Nancy Kerrigan moved up beside him and he said, "Why, yes. I'll be staying here." He turned to Nancy. "Flint is a hard name over much of the West, but I'd like you to share it with me."

"It is the man who makes the name," she said. "I am glad Flint is the name you will keep."

He thought then of a cold and bitter dawning and a lonely boy who sat on the edge of a splintery boardwalk, huddled against the chill, and of a tall man in a sheepskin coat.

"I think I owe him that," he said.

About Louis L'Amour

*"I think of myself in the oral tradition—
as a troubadour, a village tale-teller, the man
in the shadows of the campfire. That's the way
I'd like to be remembered—as a storyteller.
A good storyteller."*

IT IS DOUBTFUL that any author could be as at
home in the world re-created in his novels as Louis
Dearborn L'Amour. Not only could he physically fill the
boots of the rugged characters he wrote about, but he
literally "walked the land my characters walk." His personal experiences as well as his lifelong devotion to historical research combined to give Mr. L'Amour the
unique knowledge and understanding of people, events,
and the challenge of the American frontier that became
the hallmarks of his popularity.

Of French-Irish descent, Mr. L'Amour could trace
his own family in North America back to the early
1600s and follow their steady progression westward,
"always on the frontier." As a boy growing up in
Jamestown, North Dakota, he absorbed all he could
about his family's frontier heritage, including the
story of his great-grandfather who was scalped by
Sioux warriors.

Spurred by an eager curiosity and desire to broaden
his horizons, Mr. L'Amour left home at the age of fif-

teen and enjoyed a wide variety of jobs including seaman, lumberjack, elephant handler, skinner of dead cattle, miner, and an officer in the transportation corps during World War II. During his "yondering" days he also circled the world on a freighter, sailed a dhow on the Red Sea, was shipwrecked in the West Indies and stranded in the Mojave Desert. He won fifty-one of fifty-nine fights as a professional boxer and worked as a journalist and lecturer. He was a voracious reader and collector of rare books. His personal library contained 17,000 volumes.

Mr. L'Amour "wanted to write almost from the time I could talk." After developing a widespread following for his many frontier and adventure stories written for fiction magazines, Mr. L'Amour published his first full-length novel, *Hondo,* in the United States in 1953. Every one of his more than 120 books is in print; there are more than 300 million copies of his books in print worldwide, making him one of the best-selling authors in modern literary history. His books have been translated into twenty languages, and more than forty-five of his novels and stories have been made into feature films and television movies.

His hardcover bestsellers include *The Lonesome Gods, The Walking Drum* (his twelfth-century historical novel), *Jubal Sackett, Last of the Breed,* and *The Haunted Mesa.* His memoir, *Education of a Wandering Man,* was a leading bestseller in 1989. Audio dramatizations and adaptations of many L'Amour stories are available from Random House Audio publishing.

The recipient of many great honors and awards, in 1983 Mr. L'Amour became the first novelist ever to be awarded the Congressional Gold Medal by the United States Congress in honor of his life's work. In 1984 he was also awarded the Medal of Freedom by President Reagan.

Louis L'Amour died on June 10, 1988. His wife, Kathy, and their two children, Beau and Angelique, carry the L'Amour tradition forward with new books written by the author during his lifetime to be published by Bantam.

FORGET THE LAW OF THE JUNGLE...

The Worst
Drought In
Memory . . .

In Louis L'Amour's
classic tale
of loyalty
and betrayal . . .

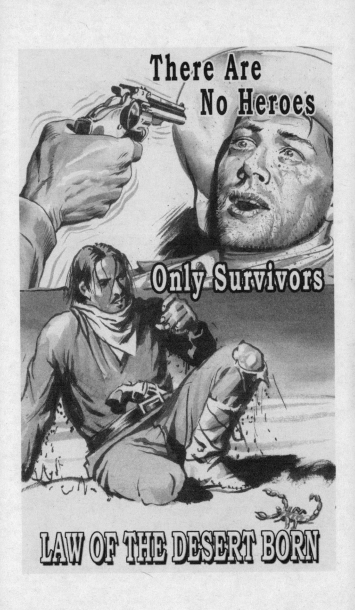

Praise for
Law of the Desert Born

"This actually may be the story's ideal form....
The result is **stunning and richly textured**."
—*Publishers Weekly*

"Yeates' artwork is **incredible**."
—GraphicNovelReporter.com

"*Law of the Desert Born* is a **fantastic**
example of how relevant the Western can be."
—Suvudu.com

"The **richer plot and characters** from
L'Amour's son Beau and collaborator Kathy
Nolan add appeal and value in addition to
the finely crafted visuals."
—*Library Journal*

"The novel's illustrations add a new
dimension to an already **gripping tale**."
—*American Cowboy*

"An **amazing level of detail and ambience**
that breathes new life into Louis L'Amour's
already stunning story."
—*Cowboys & Indians*